Ryatt

Hathaway House, Book 18

Dale Mayer

RYATT: HATHAWAY HOUSE, BOOK 18
Beverly Dale Mayer
Valley Publishing Ltd.

ISBN-13: 978-1-773365-84-8
Print Edition

Books in This Series

About This Book

Welcome to Hathaway House. Rehab Center. Safe Haven. Second chance at life and love.

After a rough start at Hathaway House and a major reboot in attitude, Ryatt still struggles to get his feet under him at the center. Seeing his sister back here hit him harder than he expected. He would like to think that, once here, he had a free pass for the rest of his life—but apparently not. Now he needs to see real progress, everlasting change, to make that future for himself that he's rather desperate to have.

Lana always looked at life with a happy, fun-loving attitude. She loves working at Hathaway and interacting with the patients and staff. It's heartwarming and rewarding work. Every once in a while she finds a patient who is reticent and even grumpy. That fits Ryatt, but she's attracted to the dark broken depths of him.

But can she show him another way to live and to view the world? She hopes so, as he's already helped her to see so much more in her own.

Sign up to be notified of all Dale's releases here!
https://geni.us/DaleNews

Prologue

R YATT STARED AT his sister. "Seriously? You're getting married?"

More change and mixed feelings slammed into him. But Quinton deserved this, and he was so happy for her. "I'm really delighted." he said. "Yeah, it kind of shook me there for a moment. You know how I feel about change and all, but this is a good change. The family needs to grow, and this is something that I think would be really good for you. He obviously adores you."

She laughed. "I don't know how that came to be, but, yes, I think you're right."

"No thinking about it. That man is unbelievably hooked."

She smiled. "Well, it's nice to know," she murmured. "He's a very special man."

"And I agree. Absolutely I would love to be part of your wedding," he told her. "Don't make it too soon, and I might even manage to walk down the aisle."

"I'm not making it too soon," she agreed, "because you can bet I'm gonna walk down it too."

He laughed at that. "Well, now we have goals," he stated. "I'm seriously delighted for you."

And, when she took off, a beaming smile took over his face. He sank down onto the bed, stunned at the turn of events. He didn't even know why he was so shocked. It was obvious that the two of them were meant for each other; maybe it was just the speed of it that shook him. And, of course, he'd just said goodbye to somebody in his life—somebody he really had no business even hanging on to—and here his sister was now making more change happening.

Ryatt wasn't very good with change; he knew that. He was working on it, but he wasn't there yet. However, he would get there. He definitely would get there. When a knock came on his doorframe, he looked up to see a small redhead, her single braid hanging down the front of her shirt. He smiled and asked, "Hi, what can I do for you?"

"Well, if you're up for it, I have paperwork for you to sign."

That was not what he wanted. He glared at her. "Great way to ruin the day."

She shrugged. "Yet it needs to be done. And I promise, afterward, I'll get out of your hair."

Pinching the bridge of his nose, he tried to convince himself that it wasn't her fault that his joy over his sister's upcoming nuptials were now a distant memory, and that reality was hitting him with a bite. "What is the paperwork for?"

"You asked for a transfer, I believe." Her tone was innocent, but a wary look filled her gaze. She set the paperwork on the small table at his side. "I'll leave these with you. When you're done, you can contact anyone in the office or bring them down yourself." And she quickly backed up to the door.

"I'm not transferring," he snapped, and his tone brooked no argument. "Yeah, I was pissed. Yeah, I was in an ugly mood, but I wasn't serious."

She stared at him, nodded, and whispered, "Got it. I'll let Dani know." And, with that, she disappeared.

Ryatt swore at his unruly bad temper, his lack of patience, and the situation that had stretched his new sense of calm to morph him into an angry bear.

Dani had called his bluff.

Good for her but not for him. He'd have to fix this.

And fast.

Chapter 1

D AYS LATER, AFTER profusely apologizing to Dani, *again*, Ryatt Metzner settled back onto his bed. He'd been at Hathaway House for two months now, maybe even longer; he'd lost track of time. And, ever since his arrival, Ryatt had been lashing out. That reaction to the changes in his life had only been exacerbated when his sister fell here, on the way to visit him, and subsequent medical tests had revealed a host of recurring medical problems for Quinton.

Her becoming a repeat patient here—out of the blue, as it seemed to Ryatt—added to his angst, as if he'd lost his way. He was finding it again, at least he hoped he was, but it seemed almost impossible to understand what had gone on and why he'd been so difficult. One part of it was hating change. The other part was not seeing a future for himself, especially after he was here in a position to heal and then suffering a mental setback when Quinton's visit required further rehab for her. It had been heartbreaking.

Yet it had also put him more or less back on track again. At least he hoped so. As he stood on his crutches, here in his room, staring out the window, a knock came at his door.

"Come in," he called out. As he turned, he saw one of the staff members, and he was pretty sure that he had sent her away in tears one day recently.

She stared hesitantly, looking at him.

"Hi." He smiled. "I'll try not to bite off your head to-day."

She flushed. "Hey, I should be used to it, but I get it. You were having a bad day."

"I was," he admitted. "Been having a lot of bad days since I got here. Still no excuse for making you pay the penalty."

"And I'd appreciate it if doesn't happen again," she noted. "I did go home at the end of my day feeling as if I'd pretty well ruined everything in your world."

"No, you had nothing to do with it." He again smiled tentatively. "I was an absolute jerk, and I'm so sorry."

She nodded. "Apology accepted. Now I'm here on Dani's request."

"Did she have to bribe you to come back here?"

At that, she burst out laughing. "Not so much. ... You do have a bad rep though."

"I'm sorry," he said instantly. "I think it's taken my sister's presence here to see the error of my ways."

She frowned, staring at him. "Your sister's here?"

He raised both eyebrows. "And here I thought everybody knew and thought everyone had already gossiped about us."

"I don't know anything about it." She frowned still. "I've been off for a few days though."

"It certainly didn't happen just over the last few days, but maybe not everybody cares."

She laughed. "Most of us have dealt with some pretty cranky patients over time, so I'm pretty sure a lot of it's been forgotten."

"Maybe," he muttered. "I don't even know how often I've seen you."

"Quite a bit," she replied cheerfully. "It breaks my heart you didn't remember." However, her bright smile belied her words.

He smirked, shaking his head. "Most people think I'm memorable, and for all the wrong reasons."

"Now you have a chance to change that," she stated firmly.

He nodded absentmindedly. "If I care, that is."

"You should care."

He tilted his head. "Why?" he asked. "When I leave here, nobody will remember me. Or, if they do, it will be for more of the wrong reasons."

"Is that how you want to be remembered?" she asked curiously. "I mean, if tomorrow were to be the last day of your life, is that how you'd want others to remember you?"

"No." He stared at her. "And I'll hardly spend every day as if it were my last."

"And yet that's what they tell us to do." She gave him an odd smile. "Make every day, … *live* every day as if it were your last because you never really know. It could be."

"That's kind of a maudlin way to go through life," he noted. She looked young for such an attitude.

"Maybe." She shrugged. "Something my mother always tried to teach me. Of course I failed."

"You failed because it's a depressing thing to remember."

"And that could be true," she agreed. "Admittedly that could be true. I don't know. I don't have all the answers."

"Why did she tell you that?"

"Because she was dying of breast cancer. Yet she struggled, and she fought, and she did the best she could to survive. Still, I think it was a battle that she knew, right from the beginning, that she couldn't win. So she finally gave in.

And I say, *gave in,* in an odd way, because obviously she didn't *give in*-give in. Cancer was just one of those things that she could no longer fight against. Her body was decaying faster than she could do anything about it." A lopsided smile peeked out. "It always made me feel bad to see somebody so beautiful and so, … so gifted being taken from us in such a senseless way."

"I think breast cancer is one of the worst diseases in the world." He shook his head, wondering at her sense of calm. "And I'm so sorry for you."

She shook her head. "Don't be, because one of the things that I did get to do was watch her go through some of the most courageous months of her life, with a grace that I know I could never even possibly equal. She was incredibly beautiful right up to the end. No, not outside of course. Her body had completely succumbed to the disease, but the person she was inside was just so beautiful that, if I hadn't had that experience, I don't know that I would be as good a person as I am today."

He continued to stare at her.

She brushed imaginary lint off her pants. "Sorry, I didn't mean to get maudlin."

"It's not even maudlin, but it's an interesting take on life. Most people aren't grateful for the horrible experiences or even realize the growth potential therein because they became a better person through it."

She nodded. "I think more people would benefit by taking another look at why this happens in their life and how they can learn from it, or maybe that's just my marketing background kicking in." She shrugged.

"From marketing to Hathaway House? How did that happen?"

"Market downturn. Layoffs. But that's not why I came to see you."

"Yeah, you never did really tell me why you are here. So, why did Dani send you?"

"Because I'm going on a shopping trip into town tomorrow. Do you need any personal supplies?"

He frowned, as he looked around. "I don't really require much. I'm okay to use whatever is available."

She nodded. "But some people want, you know, chocolate bars or a particular brand of licorice or puzzles or something to work on."

"Oh," he replied, surprised. "I never even considered that."

She shrugged. "If you think of anything, you can always call me."

"And how would I call you?" he asked curiously.

She flushed. "See? I keep forgetting that, even though you've been here for a few weeks, maybe you're not aware of how all the systems work."

"I can tell you that I'm definitely *not* aware of how the systems work, and I've been here for a couple months so far. I'm still finding my way in so many areas."

"Got it." She walked over to his tablet, brought it up, and pointed. "These are all the admins. If you need anything from any of us, you just contact us this way." She showed him a messaging system. Then tapped her picture. "That's me. I'm Lana."

He nodded. "Cool, I didn't know about that."

She smiled. "There. That's my good deed for the day." And she dashed off.

LANA WONDERED ABOUT Ryatt. He'd definitely changed. Weeks ago she'd been warned, when she had to deal with him, that he had not adapted and was one of their crankiest patients. He'd certainly lived up to his name, as he'd been angry and turning his immeasurable pain and anguish against anybody who came around him. She hadn't had the same issue necessarily, but, as she wasn't somebody who was here all the time, it made her job of popping in and popping out that much easier. Yet he was definitely nicer now.

As she walked back to her desk, Dani asked, "Do you have a grocery list for tomorrow?"

"I do. Plus I just stopped in and talked to Ryatt to see if he needed or wanted anything."

"And?" Dani asked, with interest.

Lana shook her head. "He said he's fine to use whatever and doesn't have any specific personal needs. Although he did seem surprised when I mentioned things, like puzzles and, you know, specific brands of licorice."

"How was he?"

"A very different person than I met originally." She flashed a grin. "In the week that I've been off, he seems to have improved quite a bit."

"Since his sister came around." Dani nodded. "I don't know if you know much about her, but Quinton is one of our newer patients here. She's a former patient who's back again."

"How does that work?" Lana murmured.

"For Quinton, it's a good thing, but, for her brother, I think it was a better thing." And she quickly explained about how Quinton fell here, while on the way to visit her brother.

"Ouch, that must have been hard to face that all again. Even harder to come back here, knowing how much is required to rehab. It must have seemed like going backward."

"And I think that's the good thing—in the sense that her brother may have had a wake-up call, realizing that, just because he'll do whatever he can do here, it still may not be enough."

"Interesting, but at least he's seen the light in some ways." Lana shrugged. "I know he seemed to be more thoughtful, as if thinking deeply about life."

"The more pondering he does is better for us all." Dani smiled. "So good. I'm glad you went and talked to him."

Chapter 2

LANA QUITE LIKED Ryatt. It had been tough hearing him so angry and so upset days before. But then she'd understood it because people reacted differently to the same set of problems. Before her mother had found a way to be graceful under her circumstances, she had also railed at life. Lana's father, on the other hand, had been a whole different story. He had railed and railed and railed. Even when Lana wasn't around, he kept it up.

It had been tough, watching him come apart at the seams, not dealing with his grief of losing his wife. It had been hard for all who loved them because they could do nothing for him or for her mother. Even now it was something that he didn't handle well, and it had been years since her mother had passed away. Friends and family had expected him to make at least some attempt to pick up and to move his life forward, but he hadn't. And that had been even harder to watch.

How did any parent expect their children to move on if the parents themselves couldn't? And yet that was something that she knew her dad wasn't capable of doing, at least not yet. At one point in time she had hoped it would happen, but she also had to understand where he was coming from and let it go. He was a good man, and she had worked hard to find patience and tolerance and sympathy and empathy.

But it was also hard when he didn't seem to understand that Lana also suffered in the loss of her mother and needed her father's support as well. She'd finally sought some professional help for her own grief and had come to the realization that her father would deal with his grief in his own time. All she could do was be there in a supporting role for him for as long as he needed.

Yet even her therapist reminded Lana that there was a difference between a supporting role and an enabling one.

As she worked away at her desk, she got a text message from Ryatt.

You mentioned licorice ...

She picked up the phone and called him on her cell.

As soon as he answered, he asked, "Oh, we can call?"

She laughed. "You can do pretty much anything you want—as long as it's within reason and you don't hurt anybody."

"I knew there would be a catch somewhere," he replied, with a note of humor.

She laughed. "So what kind of licorice?"

"I really love black licorice," he told her. "I haven't had any in a very long time."

"Well, we can fix that," she stated. "I just need to know a little more about what kind you prefer. I know there's soft. There are long skinny strands. There's rope licorice. There are ... one million different kinds."

"You know something? I haven't had it in so long that I don't even know what choices I have," he admitted. "Maybe get a couple different ones for me to try." And then he asked, "How does that work?"

"Tell me how much you want me to spend," she explained, "and either I can collect the money before I go or bring you a bill, and you can pay afterward."

He said, "I do have a little bit of cash but not much."

"We also can run banking through the center here," she shared. "We do that for small denominations on a regular basis for patients."

"Oh." He hesitated.

She chuckled. "Seems like you haven't quite integrated into the center yet."

"I think that's my fault," he admitted quietly. "I was so adamant that nothing here would help me that I think I hurt myself more."

"Well," she replied, "understanding that is huge progress. Now it's up to you to change it." And she added, "I'll go figure out what the black licorice choices are, and I'll bring some back this time. And we can work from there." And, with that, she hung up and got back to work.

WHEN RYATT GOT through his PT session the next day, he was tired and frustrated. He glared at Shane. "I know it's supposed to take time, but is it supposed to take this much time?"

Shane sat back on his heels, from where he'd crouched on one of the thick mats, showing Ryatt different moves. "There is no set timeline. There is no right or wrong here. PT is very individualized to accommodate each patient's strengths and weaknesses. There is no *You're doing it wrong. Therefore, you're set back,* or *You're doing it right. Therefore, you'll get out of here early,*" Shane explained. "Yes, there are definitely more correct ways to do these moves and ways that you need to do them better. You've come a long way in this last month."

"I've come a long way *emotionally*," Ryatt corrected. "And, for that, I apologize for my behavior early on."

Shane faced him again. "Good. I'm really glad you do see the change in yourself, and you understand what a problem it was before. However, the fact of the matter is, there'll always be challenges, and none of these challenges are guaranteed to be any easier. You are making physical progress. You are getting somewhere. Are you at the tipping point, where you can necessarily see it? No, absolutely not." Shane tapped his tablet. "You're at that point where it's important that we keep your spirits up, and we keep you moving forward, so that you don't get so depressed that you give up. Thankfully you have come a very long way."

"It doesn't feel like it," Ryatt replied, staring down at his twisted thigh, ending at a stump where he should have had the knee and the rest of his leg.

"You have two solid upper legs. Yet even the whole leg isn't necessarily in great functioning form right now because it is adapting while you are on crutches. You still have that solid femur bone and associated muscles on your partial leg, which will allow us to get you fitted for a prosthetic, as soon as that stump has healed. While your legs are not necessarily in great functioning form right now," Shane noted, "they will be. You've gone through so many surgeries that your body must have some time to recover and to relearn its proper function again. None of this is easy on your body. I mean, if you saw what they did during the surgeries"—Shane shook his head—"it's just amazing that the human body can recover at all."

"I wanted to see a video of each one," Ryatt confessed, "but apparently they don't do that."

"Interesting." Shane frowned, looking at him. "If it were me having that kind of surgery, I'd want to know what they did too. But, in your case, I can tell you that it was pretty rough. You've got pins. You've got staples. They would break bones and move things around in order to get them where they wanted them."

Ryatt nodded. "There was talk about some pretty rough fixes."

"Exactly, so just take it easy on yourself and don't expect more than you have to give each day."

"I haven't expected very much out of myself yet," he admitted. "I'm afraid to even look at the reasoning behind that because I feel like I've ... I had just given up."

"But that doesn't mean that you should be afraid of that," Shane stated. "You've turned quite a corner in many ways. You just need more time to keep improving."

"That's the problem though, isn't it?" he murmured. "Only so much time that I have left in that bed."

"No." Shane frowned. "We're very good at making sure that you get the time you need here," he stated. "And we don't take beds away from patients. So get that nonsense out of your head. Don't think about that as being your blocking point."

Ryatt nodded slowly. "It is definitely a concern. I mean, after seeing that my sister is back again"—Ryatt shook his head—"that was one eye-opener and not one I particularly liked to see."

"I don't think she liked it either," Shane noted, "but Hathaway House is doing her a world of good."

"Is it?" He stared at Shane. "You're not lying to me about that, are you?"

Shane stared at him in shock. "No, absolutely not. I

wouldn't do that. Lying doesn't help anyone. Not even liars trying to get away with something. And, if someone here ever lies to you, you immediately report it to Dani and to the Major. Plus, even though Quinton is your sister, you still don't get access to her medical details. If she wants you to have that, she'll give you formal permission. However, for our purposes here, dealing with you, your mind-set, your recovery at Hathaway House, I'll state for the record, in generic terms, that your sister's progressed this second time too—which is evident to all who see her around here daily, whether medical personnel, other patients, or visitors or the like."

"I didn't call you a liar—"

"Yes, you did," Shane interrupted. "And I'll call you out on every one of those negative, critical, and downright false statements that you make in front of me, until your own brain tells you to stop it. It's not good for anyone's health—yours, Quinton's, mine, *anyone's*." He stared at Ryatt and said, "Now under that veneer is the real reason you are reaching for. What is it?" When Ryatt hesitated, Shane added, "Don't waste my time or yours. Spit it out, Ryatt. Face it."

"It just worries me. I mean, what if I go through all this, and it's for nought? She's back again. Do you realize how much work and effort she put in the first time?" And then he stopped. "Of course you do. You were on her team back then, weren't you?"

"I was," Shane confirmed. "And you're right. It is disconcerting to see somebody who went through so much return again. The good news though, she will be back up on her feet in record time because of all the work she'd done before, and now we know what more we need to do to correct it."

"But why wasn't that done in the first place?" he asked in frustration.

"Just like a new car, with time and use, it wears down. And our human bodies are much more complex machines than some vehicle. We still don't know all there is to know about the systems within us. So health and healing are dynamic fields, changing as we learn more. But, in a nutshell from a PT perspective, time sometimes makes the body shift, and, in Quinton's case, she didn't recognize when her alignment was out of balance and didn't take the steps to correct it."

"So it was her fault?" he asked, confused.

"I certainly wouldn't use the term *fault*, but … definitely something changed in her physical body, and that can happen to any of us," Shane added. "It can happen to you, yes. It can happen to me. It can even happen to Quinton a third time," he stated. "It's all about doing what we need to do to stay healthy every day. And listening to our bodies. If something feels wrong, speak up, get it checked."

Ryatt nodded at that. "Fine. It's still disconcerting."

"Of course it is, and, in your case, probably a little more than we would have expected. You've seen your sister so healthy and so strong that this probably seems to you like a major failing, and I wouldn't want her or you to think of it that way," he explained.

"I don't want her to think of it as a failing at all."

"And that's good," Shane replied, "because she's done so much, all the rehab work before and again now. It's not that she's done something wrong. It's just that healing is not always 100 percent or permanent."

He nodded. "I get that. I do. It's just depressing to think

of everything that she's gone through, and here she is, back again."

"And yet it seemed to me that, dealing with her relapse, you picked yourself up and weren't quite so upset with yourself," Shane noted, sitting back. "Your attitude before was terrible, as you know, since you and I both were at loggerheads about it. However, since then, seeing your sister and what she's going through again, you seem to be better."

"And that's terrible, isn't it?" he asked, staring at him, his shoulders slumping. "Makes me feel even worse."

"Which is not why I'm saying it, but I'm asking you, how is that a thing? Explain to me how seeing your sister's setback could eventually motivate you out of your bad mood?"

"I don't know." Ryatt shrugged. "I'd just seen her for so long, supposedly healthy, but her in that hospital bed is a vision that made me really depressed, and then I got really angry."

"Anger can be a good motivator sometimes." Shane started packing up his tablet and his notepad and paper. "Sometimes anger is a really good thing. And, in this case, if it got you back on track, I'm all for it."

"Maybe," Ryatt noted, "but it's also hard because it reminds me that, no matter what she did, it still didn't work."

"You are wrong there. It did work. It worked well. For a time. Then a misalignment sent her body downhill and back here again, where we can address her alignment and set her to rights and get her back out of here again. Don't twist the facts. What I'm more interested in with you is how you managed to turn around after your sister's admittance here this second time and how you looked after your headspace when it happened to her. I still don't get that. As a PT, I'd like to know what worked for you. Maybe it would work for my other patients."

Ryatt took a deep breath. "It suddenly occurred to me that she might need more from me, more than ever before. And, while I'm sitting here and wallowing, she'd been looking after me, and now she might need me to look after her." He frowned, facing Shane. "I didn't explain that very well, but ..."

Yet Shane studied Ryatt, a smile on his face. "I think you did pretty well with that," Shane commented. "The good news is that hopefully your sister's current issues are not as bad as you may be worried about. Plus, with Stan now potentially in her life for the long-term, any worries she has will be shared."

"Is that a good thing," Ryatt asked, "to share your worry?"

"I would say so. I see it with my patients. The ones with supportive partners seem to fare better overall than the ones going it alone, unless you have a really determined young lady, like Quinton, during her first stay here. Stan's influence on her health and well-being should amplify her healing here, as he is a good person, intent on serving others." Shane looked over at Ryatt, waiting for a response.

"I know he is," Ryatt admitted. "Believe me. I do know that. I've seen him around. He brings the animals in every once in a while. Occasionally I tell him that I'm really not in the mood, and he just smiles and carries on."

"And at least you can share that with him," Shane noted. "However, it's interesting that you're not in the mood for an animal that has only love to give."

"But when you don't believe you deserve any love," he replied, "it doesn't matter how much love they have to give.

You still don't think you should be the one to get it."

Shane stared at him for a long moment. "And that is a whole different ball of wax."

Ryatt winced. "Thankfully it's not your problem. That'll be something I have to talk about with our lovely shrinks on staff." He gave Shane an eye roll.

"Maybe," Shane replied, "but *are* you talking to them?"

Ryatt flushed and glared at Shane. "I suppose now you'll tattle on me, huh?"

"No, not necessarily," he murmured, "but you might want to think about it."

"Think about what?" he asked.

"Think about talking to them about it," Shane stated. "An awful lot going on in that head of yours could use some straightening out. Giving your stump time to heal and getting a properly fitted prosthetic would help too." And, with that, Shane was gone.

As Ryatt slowly crutched his way back to his room—hating the crutches, yet acknowledging they kept him more independent—he admitted, at least to himself, how hard it was to accept help or love *because* he was depressed and fed up. … Sometimes it seemed like all this rehab was useless. His sister's return seemed to prove that—at least originally.

When he got to his room, however, he found a note on the door. *Call me.* Then he realized who it was from. He smiled, made his way over to his bed, pulled out his cell phone, and dialed Lana's number. When she answered a few minutes later, her voice was distracted. "Hey, it's Ryatt." There was a moment where he could almost think that she had blanked out on his name.

"Oh, *Ryatt.*" And then she sighed. "Ryatt, here at Hathaway. I deal with outside vendors too, so I couldn't even begin to place your name for a moment there," she explained. "It's been such a crazy day."

"Not a problem," he replied, slightly disappointed that she had no instant recognition of him by name. But then why would there be? It's not as if he'd gone out of his way to be memorable in any good fashion. "I just wondered if you had any licorice for me?"

"I'm coming down your way. I'll pop in." With that, she hung up.

He frowned and shrugged. "Whatever." If she needed to come, then that was fine. Almost instantly he pulled off his T-shirt and shifted onto the bed, groaning at the pain in his thighs after his workout session with Shane. When Ryatt looked up, she stood there, chewing on her bottom lip. He waved his hand. "Hey. Sorry."

"Sorry for what?" she asked.

He frowned. "I just ... I don't normally show pain like that."

"Maybe you should," she suggested. "It makes you a little more relatable."

He gave a brief nod, then looked at her hands. "What's that?"

"Well, you mentioned licorice." She opened the bag. "I found three different kinds, the soft Australian stuff, the regular"—and she held up a longer package—"and then these are the English type." She shook her head. "I honestly wasn't sure what you would like, so I bought one of all three. Just don't eat too much at once."

He laughed. "You know something? I'm not sure which I like either, so I'm happy to have an assortment to try."

"Good." She walked over and placed them on the night table.

"And how much do I owe you for them? I do have some cash here." The cost she noted was cheap, as far as Ryatt was concerned. "Don't you guys add a markup for having to go and collect it all?"

She laughed. "No, we sure don't. Maybe we should. Maybe we shouldn't." She gave a wave of her hand. "It's probably better for all of us if we just keep doing what we're doing."

"It's hard to run a business that way," he noted, "not capturing all that employee time, plus the gas and the wear and tear on the vehicle, right?"

"Do you know much about running a business?"

He nodded. "I took some business classes in college, and I really enjoyed them. Wanted to do more in that area," he shared. "But I quit, joined the service, thought I'd go back and finish college after my tours."

"Aha," she replied. "So is that what you'll do when you leave here?"

He frowned at her. "I really don't know. I always thought about doing some retail sporting goods shops, but not sure I'm necessarily up for it."

"You could do all kinds of stores that don't necessarily have to be retail," she noted.

"Like what?" he asked.

She shrugged. "How about a digital online store?"

"Maybe," he said. "I don't know. More things to consider."

"Well, at least you have the time to think it over." She added excitedly, "Any time you want to talk about it, I'd love to."

"Why? You like business?"

"I run a couple online stores," she shared. "They'll never

make me any self-sustaining money, but I always figured it couldn't hurt to have something as a secondary income."

He nodded. "That's very smart. Too many people never think about what comes after."

"Exactly. In my world what *comes after* was the loss of a mother, a father basically drinking himself to death, and, if I hadn't been doing what I was doing," she stated, "he probably would have taken all my money too. As it is, I'm okay, and my father, now that I've convinced him to let me handle the money, still has a roof over his head."

"I gather your father's still not adjusting to his loss."

"No, I'm not sure anybody ever really adjusts to their losses," she noted quietly.

He nodded. "Well, I'm not doing a good job on that myself, so I'm really not somebody to talk."

She smiled. "Back to that again, huh?" she asked. "You're doing fine. Just keep doing what you're doing, and you'd be surprised what you can accomplish, even given a little bit of time. Anytime you want to discuss business, I'm happy to have those conversations. As I told you earlier, I have a marketing background from my previous job, but I also have the practical real-life applications of running my own online businesses too." Then she checked her watch. "And now I need to get back and finish off too many things before my day's over."

He stopped her and suggested, "Well, maybe, one of these days, we could do lunch or something?" Immediately he backtracked. "But, of course, I know you're really busy. So, I mean, if it doesn't work, then ... you know that's fine obviously." He was astonished when he watched a real smile break across her face.

"I'd love that. Thanks. How about lunch tomorrow?"

He stared at her in shock.

"Or did you just mean some time in general?" She flushed.

"No," he replied quietly. "I'm serious. And I would love to have lunch with you tomorrow."

She grinned. "It's a good thing because now I've got all kinds of business stuff rattling around in my head."

He smiled. "I'm not against that kind of conversation. I really do love it."

"Good, we'll have lots to talk about." And, with that, she gave a little finger wave and disappeared.

Ryatt sat here on the edge of his bed, pondering what had just happened. Wasn't he just thinking about how he was depressed, how he hated the crutches, how none of this rehab was productive? What just happened here?

Shane popped his head around the doorframe almost immediately afterward. "I'm not exactly sure what I just heard," Shane noted, "but did you set up a date?"

Ryatt stared at Shane in amazement. "*Umm,* … I guess."

Shane cocked his eyebrow at him. "Because it sure sounded like that from my end."

Ryatt smiled, one that crested and took over his whole face. "You know something? I just might have."

Shane slapped the door with a big grin on his face. "Go, you." And, with that, he took off, leaving a very happy Ryatt in his wake.

Chapter 3

THE NEXT DAY, Lana couldn't wait for lunch. At 11:00 a.m. she realized that she hadn't double-checked with Ryatt about the time. She went on her computer, checked his posted schedule, and realized he was with Shane until 11:30 a.m. At that, she winced because Shane could often work his patients hard. Ryatt may not necessarily even want to go out for lunch today, depending on how serious today's workout routine was.

She hesitated when 11:30 arrived and then decided she'd better go find out for sure what kind of shape Ryatt was in.

As she walked toward his room, she hoped to find some sign that he was one way or the other. However, when she came to his closed door, she frowned. She didn't want to disturb him. She knocked gently and thought she heard something, so knocked again. When the door opened instantly, she looked up to see Ryatt there. "Sorry," she said, "I wasn't sure if you were here or not, and I didn't want to wake you, if you were napping."

"I'm here."

Obviously he was still recovering from his latest session with Shane, leaning heavily on his crutches. She looked at him in concern.

He waved away her worries. "I'm fine."

"You don't look it," she said bluntly.

He burst into laughter. "No, I probably don't, and that's just a sign of the times. How pathetic is that?"

"Not at all," she murmured. "It's pretty normal around here."

He nodded. "Isn't that the truth? However, if you give me a minute, I'll get a quick wipe down and a change of T-shirts, and then I'll be ready for lunch."

"Sounds good. Do you want me to save us a table?"

"Great. Why don't you do that? I'll meet you there."

"Sure." And she left him to it. She wasn't too sure how long he would be, but she picked a table outside on the deck, realizing that, once again, she hadn't asked him about his preferences. Shrugging, she made a choice regardless and put themselves under a big umbrella, so that they could be a little cooler, if needed. The sun could be intense here in Texas, and she wasn't sure she was up for that much heat today. It had been a pretty hectic morning for her, but what had kept her going was knowing she had lunch with Ryatt ahead of her.

"Now how silly was that?" she murmured to herself. Not a reaction she expected, particularly not to him. But he'd been very different the last few times that she'd seen him, and he had obviously turned a corner. She'd heard murmurings from everybody else around him that he was nicer now too. And they were all hoping it would last.

She knew that lasting wasn't necessarily something that was even possible, but she was happy for him. It was important to nurture the healthy mind-set and to start finding good things in life, instead of always holding back their hopes and desires, expecting to get the worst in life instead.

Yet somehow that wasn't something you could easily tell

people; it wasn't something that you could just turn around and explain to them and say, *Hey, look. If you change your attitude, your life will be that much better,* because most of the time that just made them angrier. And why wouldn't it? It would make her angry too most likely. Not exactly the mood that everybody was going for here, and so much good was being done here at Hathaway House that she was just amazed at the progress she'd seen in people. The mind really did influence the body—and vice versa too. People just had to be aware of it. Lana smiled, still amazed, overwhelmed with joy, and happy to be a part of something so special.

She'd told Dani several times how much she really loved being a part of this. And Lana knew Dani had appreciated hearing it because, as the co-owner, she'd done a great job finding other staff or people who were appreciative of the progress and could see the change happening in people's lives. That healing was … that was worth so much.

Lana was grateful she was here. And she hadn't even been here all that long, maybe six months now. It was something that she was proud to focus on, even at the end of a tedious workday, even though she might be tired, even though there might be more stress than she had been particularly ready for. Sometimes it was just nice to leave at the end of the day, regroup for a bit, and come back, knowing that she was wanted and needed here and that she was part of a worthwhile cause, part of something good for everybody, patients and staff alike.

She sat here at the outdoor table and waited for Ryatt a good ten minutes. Finally she got up and headed toward the buffet line, and, just as she did so, she saw him enter the room.

He looked at her and asked, "Am I too late?"

"No, not at all."

"Good. Shane stopped in for a minute, and that delayed me."

She nodded in understanding. "It's all good." She pointed outside to the table that she had saved for them. "I didn't know if you wanted sunshine or not."

"Today I'm tired," he murmured, "so the sun will just take more out of me than I've got to give but I'd love to catch a few minutes."

She laughed. "Good enough. Do you want to sit there for a moment and relax or come to the buffet first?"

"Let's get into line, so we don't have to wait too much longer for food."

She stepped in front of him and pulled out the trays that they needed to move along. She'd handle that, while Ryatt had his hands full with his crutches. As she did so, Dennis looked up at her and smiled. "So what'll it be?"

"I was looking for a salad. Your cooking is killing my weight."

"You don't have any kind of a weight issue at all," he said, shaking his head. "So don't be worrying about things you don't need to."

"Yeah, but, if I don't keep an eye on it," she said, with an eye roll, "it'll become a bigger problem."

At that, he burst out laughing. "Well, I won't argue with you on that point because there could be some truth to it." She smiled at him. "Anyway, how about some chicken on your salad?" At her nod, Dennis made up a vegetable salad, and added chicken and lots of feta cheese.

She stared at the salad in awe. "That's gorgeous," she murmured.

"Good." Dennis handed her the salad, which she added

to her tray.

She walked over and grabbed a juice and a small fruit salad for her dessert, chock-full of berries. With that on her tray too, she placed it on their table and looked back to see how Ryatt was doing. He was holding his own, pushing his tray along the ledge of the buffet, except his plate held twice the food that hers did. She returned to him, picked up his tray, and led the way outside.

She smiled when they got to the table. "Wow. You've really done yourself in, with that amount of food."

"I eat this much every day." He gave her half a smile.

She shook her head. "I would be fifty pounds heavier if I did that."

"I'm just trying to feed my damaged muscles, which are trying to heal. It takes a lot of protein."

"I get it," she murmured, "but it's a good thing it's you and not me. I don't think I could eat that kind of quantity."

He smiled. "You'd be surprised. I am hungry every day." Even as he sat here, working his way through his plateful, Dennis arrived with a large shake, a peculiar almost pinky-green color.

She winced, didn't know how those two colors could even go together. She looked at Dennis. And then she caught the look on Ryatt's face and laughed. "So that's more medicinal than fun, huh?"

Ryatt nodded. "Dennis keeps giving me these shakes, getting me to take this stuff, then keeps doctoring up the recipe in different forms all the time, hoping to make it palatable."

"That's because it's good for you," Dennis murmured. "It will help move you forward a lot faster. It's chock-full of greens, vitamins, minerals—all the good stuff that you need."

"I could get it from eating five more plates of this too," he murmured.

Dennis laughed. "I know you're a good eater, but not even you can eat all the whole vegetables to get all the minerals and vitamins and nutrients that your body needs right now. Bottoms up."

"You are probably right," Ryatt murmured. He picked up the shake, took a sip from the straw, tilted his head to the side as he considered it, and then he looked up at Dennis. "You know what? This one's not bad."

Dennis rolled his eyes. "None of them were bad."

"This one's great though."

And Dennis nodded, took his tray full of more healthy shakes, and walked around, handing them off to various patients.

"So does he just do this as an extra offering for the patients?" she wondered out loud.

"I think so, for anybody whose deficiencies are not being met—according to his standards and maybe the nurses and doctors and Shane too," Ryatt said in a laughing voice. "Dennis is always mixing up these heavy-duty nutritional drinks to help us get through the day."

"And that's wonderful of him," she noted, wondering at all the things she didn't know about here.

"It is." Ryatt nodded in agreement. "So many things happen here that I didn't really appreciate, not when I first arrived."

"Why were you so angry?" There, she'd done it. She'd asked point-blank what was going on in his head that told him how everything was so terrible.

"I was angry at the world, not at anyone here," he explained. "I'd just been told I couldn't have surgery to remove a piece of metal in my back, and it's something I'll have to live with. I arrived here, thinking that I would be a cripple forever and that they were only taking me on because of my sister." He laughed, shook his head, and added, "What can I say? I was an idiot. But I was just so traumatized by everything that had gone on with my accident and afterward that I wasn't willing and ready to see the good things around me."

He lifted the large glass with his odd-colored shake. "Things like this. I do tease Dennis on a regular basis because, when he first brought them to me, I was horrified with the taste, of that initial one especially. They were so rough to get down," he shared honestly. "I lost the first one. It came right back up. Dennis immediately started trying out new flavors. I'm kind of like a guinea pig here." Ryatt smiled. "And I appreciate it. I know he's trying to get me back on my feet, and maybe, just maybe, I'll make it. Yet, at the moment, it seems so far away."

"I don't think it's as far away as you think." She took a bite of her salad, paused to chew and swallow, and then added, "One of the best benefits here is the food."

He laughed. "Agreed."

RYATT HAD BEEN honest when he'd answered her questions, but afterward he wondered if he'd sounded too much like he'd been lamenting his hardships in life. Seeing his sister go through all her setbacks made Ryatt realize what a bear he was being and how ungrateful he had been for all she'd done, as well as everybody around him, who were still working to help him here at Hathaway House. It made him feel like a jerk. There was no need for it, and, even if this was as good as it would get in his life, it still wasn't the worst thing that could have happened to him.

He had all four limbs, mostly. Sure, he was missing a lower leg and, the other knee won't be wonderful anytime soon. His back had some issues, his hips as well. The muscle cramps were killing him, but, hey, they were that much better now too. Shane had done wonders on those.

If Ryatt could spend some time in the pool and the hot tub, he'd really appreciate it. However, Shane had said it wasn't on the therapy agenda just yet. Ryatt wondered if it was a reward for good behavior—something that he had to earn. Ryatt might ask about that during his session with Dr. McAdam, one of the new psychologists who visited from town all the time. That visit was this afternoon.

Later, as he sat down in the patient's chair, the doctor looked at him, smiled, and asked, "How's it going?"

"It's going better now."

"And why is that?"

Ryatt hesitated, knowing that to hide anything wouldn't be good because somebody would tattle, and yet he didn't want to share quite so much as the doctor would probably like him to. "Let's just say I had a lunch date today."

The doctor's eyebrows shot up. "Wow, not bad, considering—last time we spoke—that you were not thinking your life and your future looked very positive at all."

"I know. I know. And yet, out of the blue, I had lunch with a beautiful young woman today." He laughed. "Don't get me wrong. It wasn't anything like a date. It was just nice to know that she was there and that I could have what seemed like a normal relationship over a lunch."

"And why would you assume that nothing was there?"

the doctor asked him curiously.

Ryatt shrugged. "You know as well as I do that it'll take a special person to take on this broken body."

"Well, there is a special person who's already taken it on, and that's you. Why would you assume that there is only you in this world who's special?"

Ryatt hadn't really looked at it that way before. "I don't know. I'd have to think about that. Anyway, let's move past lunch."

"How's your attitude regarding being here?"

"Has anybody else complained recently?" he asked, staring at the doctor flatly. "I thought my attitude had changed quite a bit."

"It has," the doctor acknowledged. "And I'm sure they're all grateful for that."

He felt heat flushing his neck. "Right, I try to remind myself that they are here to help me."

"And yet you don't really want the help?"

"I just …" He stopped for a moment. "It's the same old, same old. It feels like they're doing so much, but there's only so much anybody can do, and it's like a waste of resources on me."

"Because you're not worth it?"

"No, it's not that I'm not worth it, but they're all looking for progress," he murmured. "Whereas it seems to me that this is as good … as good as it'll get."

"Have you seen your sister lately?"

"No, not for a few days."

"Is she still here?"

He shook his head. "No, she isn't. But she's back and forth quite a bit with Stan right now."

"Right. She's in a relationship with the veterinarian, isn't she?"

"Yes, and I think there's talk of them getting married and maybe her moving into his place here. Honestly I've never even considered that would be an option."

"What? That she would find a relationship?"

"No, not at all. No reason for her not to. She's come a long way since her accident."

"Right, so have you," the doctor said, turning the tables on him. "Your sister's journey is hers to deal with. You need to deal with yours."

Ryatt gave him a flat stare. "My sister's a beautiful person inside and out. I'm not. Very different circumstances."

"Ah." Doc gave Ryatt a smile. "And, of course, you believe that she has every right to and will do very well, but you don't and won't succeed because you don't deserve it. Maybe we should discuss that."

Ryatt stared moodily around the room. "Can we talk about something else?"

"Sure, let's talk about what you'll do when you leave here."

"I don't even know when that'll be. Sometimes I think it should be next week. I'm really not seeing any improvement."

"I haven't talked to Shane lately," the doctor said, "but it sounds like I should. So back to that question. What will you do when you leave here?"

"I'm not sure. Get an apartment in town maybe? I don't know. Part of me says, *Move to Hawaii and be a beach bum.*"

"Would that make you happy?"

He snorted. "No, I have a very active mind, and, even if my body isn't in prime condition, it still needs to be doing something physical."

"You could have a large garden, and looking after that would be physical."

Ryatt shrugged. "I don't think I would do well with growing things. I suspect I'd have the garden of death and weeds."

"What else would you do then?"

"I don't know," he repeated, wishing his session was over. "Maybe online businesses," he added, thinking of Lana.

"That's certainly something you can do. You're good with computers too, aren't you?"

"I'm adept at computers. However, it's not as if I'm a programmer though. Although I have some college courses in business. I never finished my program before joining up. And honestly most of that didn't and still doesn't seem relevant in my life right now."

"You are correct that you don't need to be a programmer to run online businesses. Depends on the product, I guess. Do you want to sit there and ship off product?"

He shrugged. "I really don't know. I haven't decided anything yet, so haven't thought much beyond that." They talked some more, but Ryatt felt his mood plummeting the longer he was here.

By the time he was done, he headed to his room and immediately put out the Sleeping sign on the doorknob outside, then laid down. Something was so depressing about talking about a future he couldn't see, talking about a body he didn't want to acknowledge, and seeing a today that just looked even worse than what it had yesterday.

These various psychologists were supposed to help him sort through some of his problems and get him doing better. Instead it seemed like it was a constant battle to keep himself from being majorly depressed afterward. As he lay here, his arm landed on the licorice. It brought an instant smile to his face. He reached over, opened the first package, and popped one into his mouth. It was strong and hard. He frowned, as he studied the package label, reading something about Pontefract cakes. This licorice was good, but one would be enough for quite a while because it was certainly not something you consumed quickly.

That made it a good thing then because it had time to be enjoyed. Savored almost. He thought about that, as he lay there savoring the licorice, and wondered why he couldn't also just enjoy and savor the time he was here. So much more was available to him to do here; he needed to just get out more or to find something that would release more serotonin, so that he wasn't quite so depressed all the time. And, on that note, he closed his eyes and felt himself drift off to sleep.

When he woke up again, he had an odd feeling. He checked his watch and realized that it was ten to six, and he stared again at the time, then his gaze caught the date. And he looked around in shock. He'd slept all night; he'd missed dinner and had slept all the way through. Now here it was the next morning, and breakfast was almost starting.

He shook his head in disbelief, grabbed his cell phone, and double-checked the time there. Sure enough, he'd slept all afternoon and all night. Stunned, he got up and had a shower and, at 6:30 a.m., he slowly made his way to the cafeteria on his frenemies, the crutches.

Dennis was still setting up juices and putting out fresh coffee. He took one look at Ryatt and grinned. "There you are. We missed you last night."

"Apparently I slept through dinner. I just woke up about half an hour ago."

"And sometimes it's the best thing for you," he murmured.

"I'm certainly not arguing with that. It's just odd." Ryatt shrugged. "I haven't slept like that in a very long time."

"Did anybody change your medication?"

He shook his head. "No, not at all. I was kind of down after the last visit with the psychologist—but, I mean, I wasn't *that* down."

"Sometimes all that rattling around in your brain makes you toss up things other than the contents of your stomach."

He stared at Dennis and started to laugh. "You'll never let me forget that, will you?"

Dennis immediately shook his head, grinning. "Nope, it's the only time I know of where somebody didn't keep down any food I handed them."

"Well, in this case, the psychologist might have tossed up some things in my brain but nothing useful."

"It takes time," Dennis added wisely. "Don't expect too much out of yourself so soon."

"No, maybe not," he murmured. He looked around. "When's breakfast?"

"It's coming soon. Although I've got something that just came out of the oven, if you want to start with it." And he disappeared.

Mystified, Ryatt poured coffee and waited while Dennis headed back into the kitchen area. When he returned, he had a huge tray full of cinnamon buns. "Good Lord," Ryatt said in delight. "I'm certainly not passing on those." He grabbed a small plate and took the largest one he could see. "Thanks."

With that, and Dennis's help with his food and his drink, he sat out on the deck in the sunshine, studying the sun rising through the trees and wondering at how beautiful it was out here. There was just something gorgeous about seeing green pastures and fences and horses and animals out having fun and being happy.

As he sat here, mulling over the beauty of the outdoors, his stomach was mulling over the beauty of the cinnamon bun. By the time he finished it, he had a raging appetite going on. He heard noises behind him, and he shifted carefully and noted a line forming for breakfast. That was his call. He got up, leaving his plate and cup in place, hoping that it would save his spot, and joined the queue.

When Dennis saw him coming back around again, he grinned. "So that bun was just a taste teaser, huh?"

"Absolutely." Ryatt nodded. "Now I need real food." Dennis loaded up his plate with sausages, bacon, eggs, fried potatoes, and toast. "Wow. This is perfect. I missed dinner and can handle this just fine."

"Good enough. I've got your tray and your drink, and I'll help you get settled. If you need more, come on back."

"Wouldn't that be nice? I don't think I'll be able to eat any more though." Dennis set his food and drink at Ryatt's table, as Ryatt slowly made his way around the crowd and out onto the deck on his crutches. It was harder to maneuver on them among the tables and all the people, but at least Ryatt didn't fear falling down anymore.

His seat still remained available, but several other people had joined his table. He reclaimed his chair and sat down, listening as they joked about the day coming up. He was happy to see so much joy in everybody. Several made comments about the size of his servings. He didn't say a whole lot, just dug in.

After he had eaten it all, he wondered if he'd overdone

it. So he headed back to his room to sit and to rest, before his session with Shane. If nothing else, Ryatt would warn him that he'd probably eaten too much after having missed a meal last night. Shane would understand, and, if he didn't, that's just the way it was. Ryatt could sit here and worry, or he could just get up and have another day and carry on and hope that it wouldn't be a problem.

By the time he made it to Shane's workout room for the session ahead, Ryatt felt a lot better too. And it proved to be a positive thing because he made it through his training with a whole lot more energy than normal.

Shane even noted it in the middle of the workout. "Wow, what got into you today?"

"A couple things I guess. One, I slept all last night. I missed dinner because I slept through from like three o'clock on." Ryatt shook his head. "I can't remember the last time that happened, and then, two, I ate hefty this morning," he added, "because I woke up starving."

"Interesting," Shane murmured. "Anything in particular causing the sleep?"

"Not that I know of." Ryatt focused on Shane. "I was at the psychologist's for a session right before that. I was kind of down when I came back, and then I fell asleep. And *boom*. When I woke up, it was the next morning."

"I'll put a note of it in your chart," Shane said. "Let me know if it continues."

"Why? Is it a problem?"

"Only if it's depression," Shane said quietly. "Then it's a problem."

"I've been depressed since before I got here. Yet I certainly don't want to take drugs for something like that."

"No? That's good," he murmured, "because, maybe

then, you'll work to do something about it."

At that, Ryatt rolled his eyes. Then Shane set him to do more exercises. By the time they'd finished the session, Shane sent Ryatt off to do blood work that needed to be taken. Then Ryatt made it through lunch, and the afternoon was soon done. Ryatt was tired but energized, feeling better than he had in a long time. He wasn't sure whether it was all that deep uninterrupted sleep or something else entirely, but it was the opposite of being depressed. And that was a good thing.

As he headed out onto the upper deck that evening, he wondered about going down for a walk outside on the grounds. But it was a lot of walking, and the crutches still tired him out; plus, no matter the cushion atop them, the crutches still hurt under his arms. He always had the option of a wheelchair, but, man, those were hard to move on grass or rocks.

He hated the feeling of being in a wheelchair, that overwhelming sense of insecurity and of being a victim to the circumstances—plus being so much less than a man. He knew it was all garbage; he knew it was all just mind stuff that he needed to get over because a wheelchair would certainly make getting around the grounds a lot easier.

He frowned as he stared out, wondering if he needed to do something just so that he could adjust to navigating the grounds in a wheelchair.

When a woman behind him called out, "Hey," he turned to see Lana.

"Hey." He smiled. "What are you up to?"

"I wanted to ask you that, since such an odd look was on your face."

"Oh, I was trying to convince myself that I should get

into a wheelchair and make a trip around the grounds. ... I haven't really been out exploring, and I could use the fresh air. Also I see the animals out there, and I keep thinking that it would be nice to get down there to them. But ... a wheelchair?"

"Right, I guess crutching long distances is hard, isn't it?"

He nodded. "But it's unfortunately just as hard," he added, "to force myself to think about going outside in a wheelchair for that trip."

"Sorry." She offered him a knowing smile. "However, if you want to go in the wheelchair, I'm more than happy to go out there with you." He looked at her, frowning. She nodded. "I'd prefer you went with the wheelchair, as you're a big man, and I'm not sure I could get you back here again, if you can't get inside on your own."

He smiled. "And I'm also apparently a proud man, and it's hard for me to consider going in a wheelchair."

"I guess it depends on how you want to experience the rest of your day. It's really pretty down there, and an awful lot of animals are down at Stan's, if you want to go visit."

"Maybe I should do that to begin with. I could make it into the elevator with my wheelchair."

"Then let's do it," she said enthusiastically.

He looked at her, smiled. "You don't have to babysit me, you know?"

"I wasn't babysitting, didn't mean that at all."

And he heard the hurt in her voice. He winced. "I didn't mean that in a bad way."

"Good," she said, "because that's not how I see it. I seriously do like going to Stan's and seeing the animals. He has quite a few that I wouldn't get a chance to pet otherwise."

"Okay, good. Let's go see them. I haven't made my way

down there yet."

"Oh, you'll love it."

And she seemed so honest in her response that he felt bad for even suggesting that she was doing it more out of pity. And he would have to work on that because he kept putting these negative qualities on other people, even though they didn't deserve it. He sighed, as they went back to his room and switched his crutches for a wheelchair.

"Tired?" she asked.

"I shouldn't be. It seems as if I've done nothing today but sleep and eat."

"Yet sometimes you need that."

"That's what everybody keeps telling me," he said, with a smile, leading them once more into the hallway.

As the elevator door opened, they slowly made their way into the vet clinic area. People were seated in the waiting room, but Lana walked up to the reception area. "Hey, Ryatt and I are here to see whether any animals need to go out or to be walked or something."

"Or just a cuddle," Ryatt added, with a smile.

"Well," Robin murmured, "how about you take a couple dogs outside? They need to go out into the back."

"Perfect," he said. "That sounds great." And, with that, they went outside and were handed two dogs on leashes.

"They just need a little bit of a walkaround, if you're up for it," Robin said.

Lana nodded. "That would be good." And then, for the next twenty minutes, they visited with the animals, as Lana wheeled Ryatt and led the animals around the green space closest to the vet's.

"I don't know how these animals handle all this medical intervention in their lives. We can't explain it to them, how it's for their own good, as the docs here can explain it to me," he said, after a few minutes.

"I get it. It's kind of frustrating how painful getting well can be, isn't it?"

"It sure is, but"—Ryatt shrugged—"they're doing so much better here."

"They sure are." She looked over at him, smiled. "So are you."

He stared at her. "Are you always this positive?"

"Absolutely," she murmured. "I like to smile at the world to counter all the ugliness that makes for too much negativity all the time."

"If you say so," he replied, returning her smile. "It's not that easy to change though."

"Maybe. Being happy isn't something we do instinctively. It takes time to change that mind-set, and it can take work to stay positive, even for those seemingly predisposed to it."

He nodded. "I get that. I just wasn't so sure, being around you, whether it was natural or not."

"It's absolutely natural." She laughed. "I'm surprised that you would think otherwise."

He shrugged. "Sorry, I'm not trying to be negative about it all."

"That's okay. I think it's just a challenge for me to see somebody who doesn't have the same happy mind-set I do. I guess I'm also projecting that on others. But then there's the opposite viewpoint. Like my dad. And, in a way, I'm sad for him."

"And why is that?"

"Because I the think Dad missed a lot when stuck in the negativity. I know he still does, even all these years later. It seems there's still so much going on in his mind that isn't normal and natural, and yet I'm sure he probably feels more comfortable that way because it fits his negative outlook, even though it's not really what it should be.

Chapter 4

LANA SPENT THE next few days popping in as often as she could to say hi and to see how Ryatt was doing and checking on his mood. It was a bit of a concern to know that she was interested in somebody who had a mind-set so different from her own. Yet she seemed drawn to those people, to help them, much like her persistence with her dad. Her friends told her that she had more patience than any of them would show their dads should the situation present itself.

Even in her prior job, one of the managers told Lana that she got all the difficult marketing clients because she had not only the patience and the common courtesy to treat them well, but scould even make most of them soften up, be less belligerent. To be honest, it had been a shock for Lana to hear that. No one at any of her jobs had ever mentioned it before. Yet, when Lana shared this comment with her friends, they all laughed and agreed.

"You didn't know that was your superpower?" asked her best friend Sharon, shaking her head.

Lana didn't feel powerful at all. And she wasn't sure if Ryatt's negative attitude was something that he would continue to improve or was that really just who he was. According to everybody else at Hathaway House, that's what he was like, and they had warned Lana that he wouldn't be the easiest person to get along with. She already knew that because she'd seen him at his worst in the beginning. But everybody, especially when they were down and out, had a right to be out of sorts temporarily and to not be judged for it.

People handle stress and tough times in their own way, and she wouldn't judge them or Ryatt for having a hard time getting through things. After all, he did lose a lower leg. She couldn't imagine adjusting to that would be quick and easy. But neither did she want to get caught up with somebody who would always be down and negative.

She frowned as she considered that, since it seemed she was already assessing this new relationship with him and wondering whether it had legs, so to speak.

And what was wrong with her to even think along that line? It was early days, for sure. And she wasn't the type to change another person. Yet she knew these differences could lead to problems pretty quickly. She had witnessed her girlfriends get all agog over some guy because he was different from them in whatever way. Yet, not long afterward, what was new and different and interesting became the very thing that tore apart their relationships.

Considering the future was Lana's normal thought process when first forming a relationship with a guy, but then she wasn't as experienced as many of her friends were. Lana had always had more of a discerning nature. Her friends called her "too picky." Whereas a lot of those same friends jumped into relationships, seemingly without care, almost as if the relationship jump was supposed to be this fun activity, instead of seriously trying to find somebody they were compatible with.

Lana understood that, for them, it was maybe the right

thing to do. However, for her, it wasn't. So she'd always kept herself a little bit apart. Some of her friends had teased her about it, but they had respected her decision. And even though some guys had shown a lot of interest in her, they also had turned that interest to her roommates fast enough. The fact that they were then easily interested in jumping into bed with somebody else at the same time had made it all that much easier for Lana to continuously turn down their offers.

Lana just hadn't found anybody she wanted to spend that much time with. But then apparently that was mutual, as the guys didn't waste much time on Lana or her other girlfriends either. These guys also jumped into relationships and got out of them almost as fast. She'd asked her girlfriends about it once. One had said that consensual sex was an activity to enjoy in the moment. No ties. No commitments. No other connection needed.

Lana'd just nodded, and they'd all agreed to disagree.

Yet her girlfriends continued to talk about their various boyfriends, even discussing sexual traits that each of them knew about because they'd already been to bed with the same guy. Lana had found that difficult to hear. She'd asked them, "Are you not jealous? Not upset that these guys are just going from woman to woman?"

"It doesn't matter," Teresa had responded, "because we're doing the same thing."

"Right, so as long as you all know what you and your partner are doing, nobody is supposed to get hurt?"

"Exactly," she said, smiling. "And, if you wanted to get into dating, you know a lot of guys would be interested."

"Not for me," Lana had declared instantly.

And that's where it stood today. She'd had a couple relationships that she had thought, at the time, had lasting possibilities; she'd thought that they were good to go the distance, but they weren't. And it had made her very wary over time of seeing something there that wasn't and would never be. She kept looking for somebody who was her type, her style, somebody who wouldn't be all about here and now but more about the long-term.

Back then she and her girlfriends—and their various boyfriends—had all been college kids. So a lot of youthful exploration had been involved on most people's parts. Now that Lana had been here at Hathaway House for as long as she had been, which wasn't all that long, and she'd seen the relationships here, she'd realized that these were more aligned with what she wanted. These were the relationships with staying power. Maybe she'd just been too young to hang out in that group. They weren't into the same things that Lana wanted.

That had been a lesson that she had learned quickly, and now, having found somebody she was interested in, she found herself comparing him to her prior relationships—even those of her girlfriends—and maybe that wasn't fair. Still it was almost human nature to look at him and wonder.

When she was having coffee with Ryatt one day, he nudged her gently. "Earth to Lana. Earth to Lana."

She quickly stared at him. "Sorry."

"What were you thinking?" he asked curiously.

She shrugged, embarrassed. "I was just thinking about relationships. And how so many are here. And they all seem to work. Yet those others I see—with my friends, for instance—don't work. They typically end so fast."

"Ah, but I think the reason for that's very simple."

She smirked. "Let me hear your theory then," she teased, "because I'm trying to figure it out."

He smiled. "Here at Hathaway, the people they're involved with, the half who are injured, are in a completely different space now. When life gets tough later in a normal relationship, you don't know who'll show up," he explained. "But, in a place like this, you already know who that person is. You already know the worst about them because they're here. They're already in the most difficult stage of their life. And, although they might want something different for themselves, they know perfectly well they'll have to work for it." He motioned at the building around them. "So, in a way, seeing people here is a gift because you see people at their absolute worst. Therefore, if you can live with that version of them, you then know—potentially—that the relationship's got some depth."

"And you think that out in the real world people don't show up as their true selves?"

"They don't have to," he said quietly. "When you think about it, everything is going well for them. So not really any need for their true self to show up. It's only in adversity that we're put to that kind of a test."

"And what are you like under adversity?"

"Well, I was pretty cranky to begin with"—he gave her a charming smile—"as you know."

She laughed. "If that's the worst," she said, with a wave of her hand, "that's not bad at all."

He stared at her. "I think a lot of people would argue with that."

"Ah, then they haven't been dealing with very many different people in the world." She smiled. "Like my dad, he has a temper. Yet I also knew that the temper itself wasn't the problem, as it was his way of coping with the trauma going on around him. When my mother died, that's when my real dad showed up. And it wasn't pretty. He still has a long way to go."

"And that's what I mean," Ryatt stated quietly. "If you could handle your father at that stage of his life—while already dealing with your own pain and grief—and yet can still love him, you're blessed, and he's blessed that you were and still are there for him. That's a relationship that obviously can stand the test of time."

She nodded slowly. "*Hmm.* You know what? I hadn't really thought about that relationship so much. I was thinking back on some of my college days and all the relationships around then."

He winced. "Is there anything more painful than college days?" he asked in a teasing voice.

She chuckled. "Particularly in my case because I wasn't into the whole dating scene. I was much more about making sure that I didn't waste the money that had gotten me there. Plus, I had part-time jobs on the side because I wasn't wealthy. I had to apply for student loans—and pay them back—and I had to pay for books and food myself. So going out to the pub wasn't something I could afford either. With all those issues going on around my college years, dating was just tougher."

He nodded. "But just because it was tougher doesn't mean it was bad."

"No, I hadn't thought about it as being bad. It was just a different experience for me than for a lot of people."

He nodded. "I get that, and yet people change. If you were to reconnect with a lot of those friends now, you might find that they're very different people."

"I was wondering about contacting one of them, as she lives in Houston, and I could fly down there and make a weekend trip of it. She was my best friend in college, and we've lost track. Most of the others just blended into the world."

"Interesting," he murmured. "Might be good for you."

"Maybe." She smiled. "But then again, it seems like ..." She stopped, shrugged, and finally added, "Seems like a long time ago."

"So you're afraid there won't be anything now to reconnect with?"

"Foolish, isn't it?" She checked her watch and stood. "I have to go back to work."

"Never seems to be much free time, no matter which side of the divide here."

"No, and that's because we all have something we can work on." And, with that, she turned and walked back to her office.

RYATT WATCHED LANA go. That had been a very astute comment she'd just made. Everybody had something to work on. It didn't matter how well they were doing on any side of that patient-staff divide. People could always improve on something. He wondered how he hadn't seen that before. How he'd always figured it was a *them or us* thing. And, of course, that was because he'd been playing the blame game. While he sat here, pondering, a hand landed on his shoulder, startling him. He turned and saw his sister. "Hey." He smiled at Quinton. "How are you doing?"

"I'm not doing too badly," she said, flushing with pleasure. She bent down, kissed him on the cheek. "How are you doing?"

"I don't think everybody is rushing to avoid me anymore," he admitted. "Yet I could be wrong. Just because I think I'm doing better doesn't mean I'm doing well enough."

At that comment, she stared at him and then said, "Hang on. I'll grab a coffee, if you've got a minute."

He looked at his watch. "I've got a few minutes but not too much more. Shane will come chase me down if I'm too late and make my life horrible."

She burst into loud cheerful laughter that made him grin. There was something special about his sister; she had that same bright optimism that Lana had. What Quinton had lost though, was the ability to relax. She'd always been so driven after her recuperation that she'd pretty well worn herself back down again.

He watched her, as she returned. "So what about you?" he murmured then added only half joking, "Are you doing okay? Have you calmed down enough that it's safe to be around you?"

She raised her eyebrows at him. "Wow, hard-hitting truths today, huh?"

"Yeah, I already got hit with a couple myself," he admitted, with half a smile.

"This is the place for it," she murmured. "Just when you think you have your life together, somebody comes along with wise words, and you realize that you're a long way from being together."

He laughed. "Isn't that the truth? How's Stan?" he asked in a teasing voice. And he loved watching the color roll over her face.

"He's good, and, yes, we're good too."

"Glad to hear it. It's pretty early to be having trouble."

"I don't know. It seems like trouble finds us, no matter what. It's how you handle it that counts."

"Isn't that an unfortunate fact?" he confirmed. "Still, as long as you guys are holding."

"Not only holding, we're growing." She smiled gently. "And I think that's just as important as anything else."

"Oh, I agree, and I'm working on it too. I really am." He took a deep breath. "I'm sorry I was such a jerk to you."

"You weren't a jerk to me," she countered.

He shrugged. "Well, from my perspective, it seems like I was."

She burst out laughing. "I'm not sure who is hanging out with you these days, but I think I like them."

He grinned at her. "I think you probably would too."

At that, she stopped, stared. "I saw a woman here with you, when I first stepped in, as she was just leaving."

He nodded. "Yeah, she's on staff here."

"And that happens more often than you think," she murmured.

"And why is that?" he asked, with a head tilt in her direction. "I mean, are we all so broken that we look like we need keepers? Do the keepers all need someone to look after?"

"Nope, I think that being broken is one thing, but being the kind of people who step up and do the job that's necessary? That's a whole different story. A lot of people in life are never tested. They're never given anything difficult to deal with, and, when they are tested, they fall apart. They don't have the coping skills to handle stress and stressors," she explained, "and you know we end up with some pretty horrible scenarios."

"I know. The suicides in the military are a terrible example, aren't they?"

She nodded quietly. "As is the domestic violence, when they come home."

He winced at that. "What a shock. How can you spend your whole life, waiting to be with somebody again, for an opportunity to get home to your loved ones, and then, all of a sudden, *boom!* You take them all out with you? I just can't imagine ..."

She nodded quietly. "Now that we've gone over to such a depressing topic, maybe you want to fill me in on something that's not so depressing."

"This is somewhat better but not good news. I'm not exactly progressing as Shane wants me to, and, no, it's not for a lack of trying, so don't go there."

Quinton frowned, cocked her head. "I would never say that, but I do think I remember something you shared with me early on. Shane had told you how it would take longer in your case—all because an awful lot of muscles had to be recruited to compensate for other muscles that were struggling."

He nodded. "I remember something about that too. But it doesn't change the fact that I feel like he's getting frustrated with me and that I'm not doing as well as he would expect."

"I don't think he does get frustrated with us. I think he's working with us at all times, trying to get us to do as best as we can. Then, whenever that ceiling is reached, he'll come at it from another angle," she said, with a half smile.

Ryatt grinned at that. "You know what? I can almost see him doing that. He doesn't give up, does he?"

"I don't think he gives up at all," she murmured. "And that's a good thing for us."

"And so what difference does that make overall though? Because, if it ends up being something with no ... further improvement, I still feel like I'm taking a place away from somebody else."

"Maybe, in the sense of counting beds and not having enough for the incoming patients, but you're just as welcome to have that place as anybody else is."

"But other people might deserve it more."

She let out a quiet whistle. "And here comes the root of it. You think you don't deserve it. And I bet it goes back to your accident, doesn't it? That you couldn't save Peter, even though you could save Joe, and lost part of your leg in the process."

He gave her a flat stare. "I don't want to talk about it."

"And I get it. You're fully in your rights to not talk about it."

He stared at her. "The old Quinton," he said, with quiet emphasis, "would have been hounding me for answers."

She gave him a wry look. "The new Quinton is trying to be a little more understanding and accessible."

"Is that Stan's influence?"

"Well, he's very understanding. He's very accessible, and I do feel like I have a lot to learn from him," she murmured.

Ryatt sat back, picked up his coffee cup, and stared at the contents, as he gently swirled the dark liquid. "Just because I know that I have things to deal with doesn't make them something I'm ready to deal with."

"No, definitely not, but nobody else will be ready if you're not."

"Meaning?"

"Whenever you are ready to go through that door, a lot of people are ready to help you on the other side."

"And you, did you go through that door?"

She nodded. "I did. Several times, in fact. Because, if you think that you'll go through it once and be done, you're wrong. I don't know if it works that way for some, but it certainly didn't in my case. I had to go through it and then go back through it again—because I was still messed up."

"You're the most together person I know," he murmured, having a hard time believing her. "I can't imagine you not having your life together."

She smiled. "Well, you'd be wrong. We all have stuff to deal with, and it's up to us to deal with it, as soon as we're capable."

"And if we're not?"

"I don't know. I mean, it's kind of tough to go through your whole life, hanging on to some of this stuff. I'm proof of that fact. I'd like to get rid of more."

"So what's stopping you?" he asked in a challenging voice.

"Time," she answered quietly. "I think that's what's stopping me on some of this."

"And what kind of stuff would you get rid of?"

"All those emotions tied to Mom and Dad for one."

He stopped and stared.

She nodded. "Didn't expect that answer, did you?"

"No, that's a subject that I don't talk about either."

"And because you don't like to talk about it and because it's something you avoid talking about …"

He groaned. "Then I *should* be talking about it."

She smiled. "See? You already know how this works."

"And that's because it's self-defeating talk and painful."

"And so is that kind of process."

"You know I don't want anything to do with it."

"I don't either, but it's still something I'm working on."

"And what can someone else possibly do for you?" he asked. "Honestly, I always figured that you had it so together that you had nothing left to be worked on."

She laughed. "And you'd have been so wrong because there's always stuff to be worked on. In my case I need to go back through that door of Mom and Dad again and find some things that are still holding me back, just so I can let them go."

"Do you think they ever really loved us?" Ryatt asked.

"I think so, at least in their own way. Mom loved you, and Dad loved me."

"That's kind of like giving them a free pass, isn't it? *Hey, I know you were a bad parent, but thanks for the job that you did.*"

"Well, I mean, if you think about it, they did show up for the parenting job. Individually. So we have no example of a good working relationship in a marriage. Yet, even when they were together, we never saw one hit the other nor us. They weren't addicts to smoking, drinking, or drugs. They may not have been emotionally and psychologically mature enough to be parents, but who among us really are, until we have a child of our own? Neither of us are in jail. Sure, we're both injured and broken—from running away from them to our military careers," she added, with a knowing smile. "But we aren't into drugs or on the streets or, like I said originally, in jail. So maybe they didn't do such a terrible job."

"Neither one of us has ..." And then Ryatt stopped and frowned.

"Neither one of us has what?" she prompted.

"I would say, neither one of us has a decent relationship, but I think you just fixed that, didn't you?"

"I don't know about *fixed*. However, I'm really grateful to have Stan in my life. Finding gratitude has been a huge change for me. I hadn't realized how much I was driving myself into the ground because I was afraid. Afraid I wasn't enough. Afraid that I was being treated differently or had to perform way more because of my missing leg," she explained. "And stupid stuff like that. Because there's absolutely no way that anybody at work knows about my leg. I wear pants for that reason every day." She shook her head. "And why would that be something that I have to work harder for? I was hired for my brains, not my legs."

"You already felt like you had to work harder as an attorney because you were female," he reminded her.

She nodded. "*Very* true, so that's something else that Mom and Dad are to blame for in many ways, or at least I feel like I have to work on some of those issues because of their obvious preference for their son."

He gave her a flat stare.

She nodded. "That's something we've never really talked about, but Mom left with you. You were her favorite, her pet."

He winced at that. "*Pet* is right. And since when is being a human pet in a household a good thing?"

She smiled. "It probably never is, but, in this case, it is the right word. Besides, you wanted Dad, and I needed Mom. Neither of us got what we wanted."

"I know. That's so sad too."

"Agreed," she murmured. Just then she looked behind him and smiled. "And here comes Shane."

"*Uh-oh*," Ryatt said, "now you got me in trouble."

At that, she laughed. "I'm to blame," she confessed to Shane.

He nodded as he joined them. "I saw you guys here earlier. A few minutes late is fine, as everybody needs to reconnect, and everybody needs to find that relationship that makes them give their all. But there's also a time to stop, and it's right now. He can't lose out on PT for a whole day."

"Got it." She stood up.

He looked at her and smiled gently. "You're looking better."

"Thanks. I'm due for a session in a couple days," she noted, "but I came to bring Stan some paperwork and thought I'd stop in and say hi to my brother." She reached down, patted him on the shoulder. "You just keep doing what you are doing. The improvement is very noticeable." And, with that, she turned and left.

Ryatt stared at her back as she walked away. "Do you think she meant that?"

"Well, I don't know." Shane faced Ryatt and asked, "Is your sister a liar?"

He looked at him. "There are lies, and then there are lies people say in order to make you feel better, but they don't really believe their own words."

"Oh, interesting. Is that how you see your sister?"

"No, of course not. She's one of the most ethical and moral people around."

"So then answer your own question. Do you think she meant it?"

He winced. "That's dirty pool."

Shane laughed. "No, it's making you understand that you put up all these barriers to reinforce your own lack of self-worth," he said. "Your sister loves you, but she also sees an improvement. I do too."

"What? You love me?" Ryatt asked in a teasing voice.

At that, Shane burst out laughing. "I do love that sense of humor of yours," he said, still chuckling. "It doesn't come out very often, but, man, when it does, it's good."

"Glad to hear it." Ryatt shook his head. "Honestly, it feels like even laughing is ... odd. Something I don't remember how to do."

"Maybe you don't, but we'll work on it," Shane said. "You need more of that."

"Maybe, but it's not that easy to do."

"Sure it is. It's all about letting go and finding the joy in the day."

Finding the joy in the day. Shane's words haunted Ryatt long afterward because it was also very similar to what Lana had said. Did everybody here have this secret language of how to make your day better and how to find friends and be a better friend? He didn't know. But it was something that he pondered a lot before he fell asleep.

Chapter 5

Lana noted an odd change in Ryatt's behavior over the next few days. Yet Lana could find no explanation. Finally, out of curiosity, she asked him, "So, I couldn't help but notice. These last couple days, you've been a little different."

He stared at her. "Have I?"

She nodded. "Yes, you have."

"Well, maybe it was because of my sister's visit."

She tilted her head, frowning at him. "Right. This is the sister I've yet to meet."

"And I don't know how you could have missed her." He laughed. "She is pretty special. While she is not here all that often, however, when she is—well, I don't know how to say it—it's like maybe a breath of fresh air walks in the door with her."

She stared at him for a long moment. "That is a lovely thing to say. I hope you say things like that to her face. It would make her day too."

He laughed. "She's already saying that I look and sound different, and she's trying to figure out why."

"Of course you are different, and it's … it's good. I'm really thrilled for you."

"And how do you even know what progress I've made?" he asked in a teasing voice.

"I see it every day, when we meet for coffee or lunch or whatever. However, because you are so focused on your physical injuries and shortfalls, which Shane's probably measuring every day, I don't think you see the improvement. I don't think you notice and track your own moods and behaviors on a regular basis the way I do."

"No, self-introspection isn't necessarily something I'm very good at either."

"Oh, I think you'd be surprised. I think you're better at it than you expect."

He shrugged. "Well, I mean, if I keep believing it, maybe I'll work on it."

She smiled and had to be content with that. Yet she was hoping one day that she could meet this sister.

AFTER HER WEEKEND off, Lana walked to Ryatt's room to hear him laughing and joking on the phone. With his door open, she had just witnessed another side to him that he needed to bring out more. When he got off the phone and saw her there, a big smile formed on his face.

"It was my sister again."

"Are you sure she even exists?" she asked in a teasing voice. "I'm pretty sure you just made her up."

He shook his head. "You'll have to meet her sometime."

"I'd love to," she said instantly. "She sounds like a wonderful person."

"She's definitely that. She's also different, unique, injured, and back here again working with Shane—first from a bed here and now as an outpatient."

"I heard that, and maybe I have seen her but just didn't

know who she was."

"Most likely." He nodded, with a smile. "Next time she's here, we'll have a meal or coffee together."

"Sounds good." Lana hoped he meant it.

SEVERAL DAYS LATER Lana looked up to find an unknown woman standing in the doorway to her office. With a polite smile, Lana asked if she could help her.

The woman gave her the gentlest of smiles. "My name is Quinton. Ryatt's my brother."

"Oh my." Lana jumped to her feet, came around, and went to shake the woman's hand but was swept by Quinton into a big hug instead. "Nice to meet you," Lana said, when she could, pleased to sense such an immediate acceptance. "Is that hug," she asked in a teasing voice, "because I'm still friends with your brother or because you need something?"

Quinton laughed out loud. "Anybody who can put up with my brother deserves a hug. He can be quite insufferable."

Lana laughed. "He can be, but I've also seen some blessings in his behavior too."

"Especially lately," Quinton confirmed. "I wondered if that was you."

"No, it's him," Lana said, frowning.

Quinton shook her head. "I just meant, if it was the effect of having you in his life."

Lana shrugged. "I don't know. I don't even know what to say to that. But I do enjoy spending time with him."

"Good," Quinton said gently. "I just wanted to introduce myself and to say, *Sorry we haven't had a chance to meet before today.* And I am on the run right now," she explained, "but maybe next time we can have coffee." And, with that, she was gone.

Lana thought about Quinton's words a lot over the next few days, as she worked on a big PR plan to share Hathaway House's rehab options and successes to both referring doctors and patients wanting more improvements. She loved marketing, and it was refreshing to work on this project and to build up the center's online profile.

Her own home businesses were small, but still it was amazing how much she'd learned about the digital world just from being involved firsthand. Even just studying websites known for their award-winning designs, for attracting new visitors daily who then became new sign-ups. Her marketing background helped get Lana's small online profile growing. She did ads for one company and did PR work for small businesses. Thankfully Dani didn't have a problem with Lana keeping these other income sources flowing, as her skills could only enhance her work at the center.

During a break a couple days later, Lana told Ryatt about Quinton popping in at Lana's office to meet her.

He nodded. "That would be her. She's very outgoing, and, once she knew that you were here and were interested in meeting her, she'd have been there in a heartbeat."

"Well, she seems like such a lovely person."

"She is." And he left it at that, then pointed at his watch. "Can't keep Shane waiting."

Between Ryatt's full-time rehab schedule and Lana's multiple jobs, she didn't get to see Ryatt as much as she would like. She felt that Ryatt would agree with her there. Still, even being crazy busy, she noticed Ryatt was kind of emotional over the next few days. Finally she couldn't contain her curiosity and brought it up. "I'm always asking what's going on in your world, but it seems like something else has shifted with you again."

He stared at her, an odd look on his face. "My sister's dealing with some family stuff, which then triggered some stuff for me." He gave a wave of his hand. "Once that initial trigger happened, it just triggered more stuff."

"But you're dealing with it?"

He nodded. "I'm trying to."

"I gather you have a great relationship with your sister?"

"Absolutely I do, but neither of us had great relationships with our parents."

She winced at that. "I don't think there's anything more important than a parental relationship, and yet so many of them are dysfunctional."

"Yeah, that's one word for it," he stated, with half a smile. "Our folks were dysfunctional in so many ways. And it's sad because it affects all of us for so long, and it just seems so unfair. And you? ... How are you doing, after losing your mother? It must have been tough."

"You never can plan for death. An instantaneous death must be such a shock. Yet, even knowing my mother was dying of cancer, I was still not prepared for it. My mother was sick for a long time, so, in many ways, her death was a release. Yet feeling like it was a release also made me feel guilty—because it seemed like it was a betrayal that I wanted her gone. And, of course, I didn't want her gone, but she was in such pain, and I did want her to be free of that. When her body gave out, nobody could do anything more for her. But it was ... It was so painful, so sad," she murmured. "The physical separation hurts so much, but eventually I found peace within, as I carry the memories of her with me forever.

And, with time, I have more good memories than bad."

Ryatt nodded. "It was different for me. I was definitely the favorite in the family because I was the boy, yet there wasn't a whole lot of joy in the family. When things get ugly, it takes all the joy out of life. I wasn't planning on ever dealing with it, but my sister brought it up, and I kind of felt like I needed to confront it too."

She smiled. "You know something? I'm really proud of you for that."

He stared at her. "Why? You say the darndest things." When she just continued to smile at him, Ryatt shrugged. "I come from a world where not many people say anything nice. You are a breath of fresh air. So thank you for being you."

The next week Ryatt spent as much free time as he could with Lana, while trying to avoid Shane in the common areas. Not on purpose necessarily but, every time he ran into Shane, it reminded Ryatt of that sense of failure he had in his PT sessions and how he was afraid that he would be sent away because he just couldn't do as much as Shane thought he should do.

Finally Lana asked him calmly one day, "What are you trying to avoid?"

"What are you talking about?" he asked.

"Every time I see you, you're almost furtive, as if you're trying to avoid someone."

He winced. "That obvious, huh?"

"Yep, that obvious. What's going on?"

"I just feel like, since I'm not getting the progress that I should be, I'm afraid they'll ask me to leave," he admitted finally.

She stared at him in shock. "I don't know if they do

that."

"I think they would have to from a financial standpoint," he murmured. "When you think about it, Hathaway House is still a business."

She nodded her head slowly. "I guess it is at that. I don't know of it happening to anybody yet."

"And I don't want to be the first one," he muttered.

"But still, wouldn't you then want to see Shane to find out if there's more that you can learn and do?" she asked quietly.

Her voice, her tone, got him. He looked over at her. "I've thought about that," he replied, "but I don't know what else I can do. I figured, if I brought it up, then it's just putting it in their heads."

She snickered at that. "I'm pretty sure, if it's something that they're prepared to bring up, it's already in their heads."

He winced. "And that just makes me feel like a bigger idiot after all."

"No, not at all. The fact that you're worried about it means it's something you need to bring up because that worry alone is holding you back."

Ryatt stared out moodily. "It is eating me up."

"Then do something about it. Remember. This is your life. You need to grab hold and make it what you want it to be."

Something was so positive and inspiring about everything she said, yet it made him feel worse. Instead of being inspired, he had a horrible feeling that he was failing her and himself. He nodded absentmindedly but wasn't sure how to proceed.

She didn't mention that conversation again, yet it felt like she was waiting for an update from him, and that too was eating away at him.

After a terrible night, he knew he had to do something at the next session with Shane, before they got started. "So," Ryatt asked, "if I don't get any more progress, do you ask me to leave now?"

Shane looked up from the tablet in his hand and studied him carefully. "Do you want to leave?"

"No," he said instantly. And then he frowned. "I feel like I'm avoiding you because I'm afraid you'll ask me to leave."

"Wow." Shane sat back and stared at him. "I have yet to ask anybody to leave."

"Which is kind of what somebody told me"—he stopped for a moment—"but it seems to me, if I'm not making any progress, then I'm a bit of a fraud, and you need people here who will improve. So, if I can't be that person," he added, "I figured that I wouldn't be allowed to stay."

At that, Shane put down the tablet and hooked his arms around his knees. "Wow. Again with the things that we can get our brains all twisted up about."

"And honestly, I wouldn't even be asking, except that I told Lana that I would. And it feels like she's waiting." He gave Shane a crooked grin.

"I'm glad to hear that Lana's got some sense." Shane shook his head. "You are showing progress. You just haven't hit the tipping point yet."

"It doesn't feel like I'm showing *any* progress." He shot Shane a hard look. "And I figured for sure then the bed needed to go to people who could improve."

"This isn't a competition. This isn't a case of you need to do better in order to stay here. That's not how this works. The only possible competition is with yourself. Being better now than you were before."

"Maybe I'm not," Ryatt murmured. "That's how it felt."

"I'm sure it did, and I'm glad you brought it up. Too bad you didn't a week or so ago."

"Hey, well, it's kind of hard to figure out this mess. There's just so much that's wrong in life. It's hard to know at what point in time I'm putting the idea in your head."

At that, Shane started to chuckle. "Is that why you didn't ask? Just in case I hadn't thought of it, and I would take this opportunity to get rid of you?"

Ryatt had the grace to look ashamed at that. "Maybe," he muttered. "And I know it sounds stupid, but you know how this works. Once a worry like that gets a hold …"

"Once it gets a hold," Shane said, shaking his head, "it's everything. It dominates your thoughts to the point you can't think about anything else."

"Exactly," he muttered. "Which is also why I'm asking."

"And I'm glad you are, and the answer is no. We won't get rid of you. No, there isn't a rule where you have to show enough progress in order to stay. And the sad fact is, *you* don't see *your* progress, and that's something we'll work on today," Shane stated.

"What progress?"

"Exactly. For you to see the progress, I can do a few things. I was waiting until you improved a little more, so I could show you how this worked," he explained, "but obviously you need to see it now."

"You know what? Even if it's a little bit improved, it would make me feel better, and just saying that makes me feel stupid."

"I don't even want to hear that," Shane muttered, "because that's not the point of this." And, with that, he added, "We'll do a series of exercises, and I'll record it, and then I'll show you the results."

What followed was a session like none other.

"Now we'll do a spine movement, then core, followed by abs and glutes." And it went like clockwork, one after the other, after the other.

"Most of these are pretty easy though," Ryatt noted.

"Exactly. But they're also exercises that we did a couple months ago, when you first started here. And so, although the progress has been slow, remember how I told you that it would take longer for you to reach that tipping point? All because so many muscles had to be recruited to kick in to do the job correctly. So, in theory, you should see *some* progress today, with what I'm about to show you, even if you don't see a lot."

When they were finally done, Ryatt had worked up enough of a sweat that he lay here on the mat on the floor. "Okay, so I take that back. It feels like that was a hefty workout at this point."

Shane nodded. "Now give me a few minutes," he said, as he worked away on the computer.

"What are you doing?" Ryatt asked.

"I'm bringing up the video when you first started here," Shane replied, furiously clicking the keyboard. "I ran you through a bunch of tests, not necessarily these we did today in particular, but you should still recognize the difference when you compare the two."

Ryatt wasn't sure what Shane was talking about, but, all of a sudden, he had the screen up, split in two, each feeding in images. "Now watch this." Shane hit Play in one of the screens.

And Ryatt watched the video taken early after his arrival here at Hathaway House, when he'd first got here. He winced as he saw the gait and the pain on his face and the little bit he could do. Not to mention the massive effort he had to put in to achieve those moves. "Wow, I really wasn't doing very well, was I?"

"Nope."

In fact, it looked painful just even watching. "Everything he does hurts," he muttered.

"Yeah, and that's what you were like, back then. Now watch this." And now Shane had both screens playing.

Some of the exercises were the same, some were different. They were definitely more advanced. But even as Ryatt watched today's workout on tape, he saw that he moved with a freer, more relaxed rhythm, that his body responded to the instructions with much less hesitation. Now every movement shifted and flowed in a smooth manner and with much less effort.

He muttered a curse word under his breath, frowning.

"That's what I'm trying to show you," Shane said. "There is progress, not as much as you would like to see, and I get that. We're always impatient for progress, but, in this scenario, it's definitely visible. It's more visible now that I look at it again," Shane added, as he studied the videos. "I'm glad we did this. I will have to remember to do this a little more often."

"Do what?" Ryatt asked curiously.

"Show the now-and-then feedback, like this. It's easy to get caught up in everything that needs to be done, and we don't really think about the importance of the patient seeing improvement, as long as we, the medical personnel, see it. You guys need to see these milestones as they happen. There's not always the same positive results for everybody, but, when they happen, it's really important that you guys can *see* that kind of progress and can feel it. You guys put in a ton of effort, a lot of hard work on a daily basis. And, if you don't have that kind of feedback, I'm sure it must be difficult to keep going."

"It is difficult to keep going," Ryatt acknowledged, "because I felt like I wasn't getting anywhere. I was honestly terrified that I would get kicked out."

They talked a bit longer, and, when Ryatt was done questioning Shane, Ryatt had to admit he had a new lease on life. Even when he showed up at lunchtime in a wheelchair, he positively beamed. As he pushed up to the table and to a huge plate of food in front of him, he rubbed his hands together in joy.

Dennis came over and grinned. "Well, I've seen lots of happiness on your face, yet I'm not sure what's going on now, but enjoy dinner."

"I will. I haven't had a good steak like this in a long time."

"You must have missed our last steak night. That's too bad."

"That's okay. I'll make up for it now."

Dennis burst out laughing. "You do that," he said, as he walked back to the kitchen.

When Ryatt looked up again, Lana headed toward him, grinning.

"I'm not sure what put that smile on your face, but everybody is talking about it," she said.

He chuckled. "What put it on my face is the fact that you were right."

She stared at him. "Right about what?"

"About talking to Shane."

"*Ahhh.*" She grinned. "Well, that's good. I'm glad he was

able to put your fears at ease."

"Do you have to say, *fears?*" He wrinkled up his face. "Makes me sound like a two-year-old."

She snickered. "Well, if the shoe fits."

He groaned. "Okay, so it was definitely on the immature side. Sorry about that."

"No, it's a heck of a good lesson to learn now because I'm sure there'll be a lot more issues over the next few months that you're here, so I wouldn't worry about it. At least you got to the bottom of it, and now you know where you stand. And, by the way," she added, "where do you stand?"

"He did a video of my workout today," he said enthusiastically. "And then he showed me a video of when I first arrived. And it wasn't even so much what he said as much as I could *see* the progress for myself."

She beamed. "See? That's even better. Not only do you no longer have to worry about being kicked out, but you're also doing so well that you can see that progress yourself."

"It's kind of weird that I didn't see it."

"Does there have to be a why?"

"I don't know. I guess I was just too close to the trees to see the forest."

"That works for me," she said quietly. "It happens to all of us, you know? Even on a new job, you do the best you can, and it seems like, for a couple weeks or so, everything's fine. Then absolutely everything possible goes wrong, and you think, *Oh, I'm doing the worst I could ever do, and I'll get fired at any moment.* Then, as things calm down, you realize that really you're doing okay. It's just you had a couple bad days."

"I always figured it took a good six weeks to get used to a

new job anyway," Ryatt murmured. "And you're right. After everything goes wrong in that time period, you're sure, absolutely positive, that you'll get fired."

She grinned. "Yep, that's just life. The important thing is that you talked to Shane. You went and did something about that fear."

"But I didn't," he said ruefully. "Not until you brought it up."

"And I'm proud of the fact that you listened to what somebody else had to offer, and you saw the value in it and followed through," she replied.

"Are you always so"—he shrugged—"nice?" She laughed out loud, the beautiful sound pealing across the deck. He saw other people turning to wonder what was going on in Ryatt's and Lana's world, as if maybe those onlookers wanted to have some of that same sunshine themselves.

Ryatt grinned. "I didn't think my question was that funny."

"Oh, it was." She nodded, still chuckling. "And I'm not always like this. As you well know, I also have bad days."

"Well, if anytime you've had a bad day since I've been here," Ryatt noted, "I never noticed it." She shrugged. "Just because it's a tougher day doesn't mean I get to bring down everybody else's day because of it."

He winced. "Ouch, that feels like another direct hit."

"Not at all," she said firmly. "I'm not the kind of person to send out direct hits."

"No, but your words are a whole lot more effective because of it." Ryatt stared at her, fascinated. "It makes me feel like I have to step up to the plate. Otherwise I'll disappoint you," he murmured.

She looked at him. "Well, here's the thing. It's not like

you should try to avoid disappointing me," she noted, "because that's not what our relationship's all about." She smiled. "You have to do what you need to do so you don't disappoint yourself." And, with that, her phone rang. She held up her cell. "I've got to get back to work. I've been expecting this call." And she quickly dashed off.

Leaving him wondering, once again, at the wisdom that seemed to be so profound and so plentiful in this place.

Chapter 6

W HEN LANA ARRIVED at work the next morning, Dani was waiting for her. "Problems?" Lana asked.

"Always." Dani gave her an eye roll. "Yet nothing more than usual."

"Oh, good. You had me worried, when I saw you standing there."

"Worried about what?"

"Getting fired," she said, with a big grin. "It's always a concern."

"Not here. If there was ever a problem, I'd give you a warning. You know that, right?"

"Thanks, and I would assume that." Lana nodded. "But not everybody is as kind as you are."

Dani laughed. "Kind or not, I've still had to move out people sometimes. However, with you? I need that fresh eye you offer."

"Have you ever had to ask patients to leave?"

"Yes, just not very often."

"It was a concern for Ryatt. He figured that, with no progress, you would ask him to leave."

Dani's jaw dropped. "Oh, wow. I wonder where he got that idea from?"

"I don't know, but it was certainly a concern. He did talk to Shane about it though, so I'm really happy that Ryatt got it resolved—in his head at least."

"I am too," Dani said. "That's not the type of mental confidence that we need them to have. It's tough enough being here without being afraid that, if you don't do enough or if you don't make the grade, you can't stay."

"That's why I told him to go talk to Shane, to make sure that that was put to rest before it became an even bigger issue."

"Absolutely." Dani shook her head. "No, it was that meeting yesterday that brought me here. Did you take some notes? I was supposed to, but I apparently got so caught up in it that I didn't."

"I took some notes, but we really should just ask them to send over a recap of bullet points or whatever at the end of every meeting."

"We should, but there's just so much going on sometimes that I don't know if any of us remember to ask for that."

"Then maybe we need to appoint somebody as corporate secretary to Hathaway House and to attend certain meetings, specifically just to take notes."

"Good idea," Dani muttered. "As the center has grown, still Dad and I remain the only corporate officials in charge."

"Which means it falls to you," Lana added, handing off the notes that she'd put down on paper. "Not a whole lot here though."

"That's fine," Dani muttered, as she scanned it. She tapped the page. "Here. That's what I was looking for." She wrote down a number, leaving Lana's notes with her. "Thanks." And, with that, Dani was gone again.

As Lana sat down, she realized just how much her own insecurities were always at play because, when she'd seen

Dani like that, upset and not in the normal Dani type mood, Lana had immediately worried that something was wrong with the job Lana was doing. She could hardly blame Ryatt for being concerned, when she'd fallen into the same trap herself. Still, thankfully that wasn't an issue now because she'd brought it up right away with Dani.

As Lana went about her day though, she wondered just how much these kinds of insecurities affected everybody at the center. She wondered if it was something they needed to make clearer at staff meetings in general and at patient and staff relationship meetings specifically. She brought it up to Dani later in the day.

Dani stared at her. "You know what? After what you said about Ryatt, I was thinking the same thing."

"And seriously my own insecurities too, when I saw you there, standing at my office this morning. My instinctive first thought was that I was being fired."

Dani whistled. "Isn't it just amazing how the mind immediately goes to a trauma and can't figure out any other way to see itself clear?"

"It's kind of rough though because it's not how we would want to deal with issues and certainly don't want the patients to have that added stress either."

"No, of course not," Dani agreed. "And I think you're right. I think we need to add it to the staff training to ensure that patients understand that they're not on … what? … What is it I want to say?" she asked, staring off in the distance.

"They are not on sufferance or probation and, while they are expected to put forth the effort to improve, that they aren't expected to *perform or else*," she murmured.

"Yes, exactly. Can you write up a brief summary of those

ideas? We'll send out an email as a reminder."

"Oh, that's a good idea too."

THE FOLLOWING MONDAY, Shane popped in and asked Lana, "Was that your idea?"

"What?" she asked, staring at him, confused.

"That email about the staff ensuring the patients feel like they were not on a probationary testing ground here."

"Yes," she muttered. "At least somewhat of an idea. Dani and I were both talking about it."

"I presume Ryatt brought that up."

"Yes and no. I came in the other day, and Dani was standing at my door, and I immediately worried that I was being fired," she said. "It brought up that, if it was happening to both Ryatt and me, maybe a whole pile of other people feel that way too."

"Well, several other people have brought it up now that it's been addressed, so good call on your part." And, with that, he was gone.

She smiled. It's the one thing that most people here were really good at—they gave credit where credit was due. And, for that, she was quite happy. At least whenever she put up a suggestion somewhere, it wasn't knocked down as being stupid or too ... useless or whatever. She remembered a few times in her previous marketing job where she had similar problems, where anything that she would suggest would be shot down because it wasn't relevant, because it wasn't a good idea. She'd started to get a bit of a complex out of it.

However, she'd found out fairly quickly how different it was at Hathaway House. And she was grateful for that; it made a huge working environment difference. Plus, she was starting to really care about Ryatt and to see him take steps to make changes. That was everything. She herself needed to keep up with him. Otherwise he would pass her, and she'd feel terrible. Here she was telling him to do something, and, if she wouldn't do it herself, that didn't make any sense either. She was still pondering that, when she met him for lunch.

"Now that's a pensive look on your face," he said in a teasing voice.

"And you're still in a high-spirits mood."

"Hey, my session went well today. I'm not in a ton of pain. I can see progress." He had said it with such relish that she laughed out loud.

"I love that. I really do. That's just amazing that you're doing so well. I was thinking about that today. Like here, we're talking about you making progress, and I was thinking of all the things in my life that maybe I needed to make progress on. Otherwise you'll pass me by."

"What's this? A competition now?" he asked in a teasing voice.

"No, not at all. There is that sense about wanting to make sure that I do something worthy in my life too."

"I think working here would be quite worthy enough. You are helping so many people."

"I wonder," she murmured. "Did you put any more thought into what you'll do when this is over?"

"Not a whole lot yet. Trying to keep the stress down."

She nodded. "Yet we've talked about home businesses several times."

"And I keep thinking about it," he said. "I'm not sure I'm ready for a solid indoor job. I'm used to being physically active on the job, so I'm not quite ready to just become a computer nerd."

She grinned. "You see? That's the kind of thinking that you need to do, to sort it out now, so that when you do whatever retraining, if you need retraining," she added, "you pick something that you'll be comfortable with, long-term."

RYATT WASN'T EVEN sure yet what he wanted to do long-term, but the fact that she'd brought it up also made him realize that he was getting comfortable here now, and it was probably time for him to get uncomfortable with that comfortableness. To be sure that he did consider what his future was and that it didn't sneak up on him with the suddenness that everything here seemed to. An amazing amount of time had whipped past that he felt he needed to push forward and to consider some of his options.

When he was at the next shrink's visit, this time with Dr. Sullivan, she told him, "I'm hearing good things about your PT progress."

"Yes." Ryatt gave her a fat smile. "And I'll tell you that it feels really good to know that that's happening."

"Of course it does. So what else is on your mind these days?"

"My future," he responded bluntly.

"Good call," she replied. "That's definitely facing you."

"I know," he agreed, "and that's hard too because I'm not exactly sure what I want to do."

"I don't know that you have to decide right now, do you?"

"No, but I'd like to think that I'd have some idea, some

inkling of where to go from here, before actually leaving Hathaway House."

"If you're ready to find out that direction, then great, but that doesn't mean you should force yourself. Not yet."

"And mostly I don't feel like I am ready for the future focus," he said, "but then I'm reminded of how much time has gone by and so fast that I almost panic and worry that I need to make a decision now."

"And I don't want you feeling like that," she said. "You already have stress issues. Doing something like that could just make it worse."

"Maybe," he muttered. "It does seem to be a bit of an issue right now. Every once in a while I'm reminded that my time is passing so quickly and then *boom!* I start to worry."

"Right," she agreed. "But, at the same time, as long as you're thinking about it, and you're open to options, I think that's all that's required of you at the moment. And what are you thinking about, as far as options go?" Only simple curiosity filled her voice though. No judgment. No pressure.

He shrugged. "I was contemplating some online businesses. But I'm not sure I want that kind of a sedentary lifestyle."

"Does it have to be sedentary? It seems like everybody does things from their phones all the time these days," she suggested.

He stared at her. "I don't know why I didn't think of that, but you're right. So much of business is just done on the phone, and I could certainly do that, while out and about." He pondered it.

"And what kind of business?"

"I'm not sure. I was wondering about buying a business or just setting up something simple online or maybe a couple digital companies."

"Most people start with one," she noted, laughing.

He grinned. "I'd set up a couple and hope to get lucky on one. If I can get into the right business, it could be good."

She nodded. "Well, if you understand what you're doing," she noted, "you're ahead of the game already."

"Understanding what I'm doing and doing it right are two different things. I don't have any practical business experience, but I'm willing to learn, and I'm a fast learner. Plus, I have some money set aside to tide me over, until I get a business up and running."

"And that is a huge blessing," she stated, with a nod. "I don't even know that you realize how much of one."

"Probably not," he admitted, "as it's been brought home to me time and time again that I don't really see myself quite the same way that other people do."

"And I think that's true for everyone," she added, with a smile. "Yet it sounds like you've already got some of this figured out."

"Some of it, yes," he agreed, with a lopsided smirk. "I just don't know quite what the finished look will be."

"Does it matter?"

"In some ways, yes." He hesitated and then added, "I get that, for some people, it probably doesn't matter how well I end up on the physical spectrum, but I would like to be the best that I can be, and I want that to look very close to normal."

She settled back. "And why is that?"

He looked at her and shrugged. "I don't know that a *why* is in there," he replied in confusion. "I just know that I'd like to be as close to normal as I can be."

"And yet you say, *normal,* as in, you don't say, *as good as you can be."*

"Well, I said that first." He stopped, then frowned. "Now you'll tell me something is wrong with the way I worded it."

"Not so much that," she explained. "I just want to make sure, whatever it is you're looking at doing, that you do it for you and not for somebody else."

At that, he got her meaning. "Meaning that I want to be normal so that other people see me as normal?"

"That's my question to you. Why is *normal* the important part?"

"I guess so that I don't feel like I'm different," he murmured. "That I'm as good as, if not better than"—he shrugged—"I was before. I'm as good as anybody else. In fact, in certain military terms, I'm better than most. I was always a strong, fit healthy male, and I'd like to get back to that."

"Good," she said. "Getting back to that sounds like a great idea. Just make sure you're getting back to it and not trying to become it just so that you can look good."

"Isn't that the same thing?"

"No, not at all. One is you regaining something that you had at one point in time—that healthy, strong, physically fit body. Another one is so that you don't end up looking other than normal," she murmured. "As if you're trying to do it for somebody else."

"Ah, so back to that needing to do things for the right reason."

She nodded. "It's very important, particularly when it comes to your healing."

He winced. "And every time I take a step forward, it seems like I'm sliding even further backward."

"Not at all," she said warmly. "You're making incredible progress. Don't ever forget that."

"Now you sound like Shane," he murmured.

"Does that matter?"

"No. Maybe not. Everyone here is always so positive, so encouraging, that it surprises me sometimes. But you've definitely given me something more to think about."

"And something more to think about is huge, so mull it over, and we'll talk more about that next time too."

Chapter 7

I T TOOK SEVERAL more days of understanding where her own fears were coming from for Lana to verbalize it to Dani. She stopped in and announced, "It's just fear, fear of not having enough."

Dani looked at her in surprise. "Pardon?"

At that, Lana chuckled. "Sorry, a little preamble would have helped."

"Or at least a bit of notice as to what the conversation was supposed to be about," Dani suggested, "although it sounded interesting."

"When my first instinct, seeing you waiting at my office, was that I was being fired," she replied, "it goes back to that whole fear of not having enough."

"Ah." Dani nodded. "That makes a lot of sense. Nothing quite like knowing that survival is still something that's ever at the forefront for anyone. And, when we lose something pertinent to our survival, how messed up we can get so very quickly."

Lana nodded. "Good point," she agreed, "and definitely something that I think we should consider for staff training considerations, even if it doesn't extend to the patients as well. It just might be helpful to bring it up at some point in time for the employees to consider in their own worlds. Obviously my case is different from your case. Our situations are different."

"True. I understand," Dani replied. "Nothing like running a center like this and having so many people's livelihoods in your hands to make you realize just how delicate of a situation the success of Hathaway House is for everyone."

"You're quite right there. I'm just trying to keep myself afloat. I can't imagine being responsible for all these other people around here." Lana shook her head. "And, of course, that's what you deal with all the time."

"Most of the time it's fine, and then, every once in a while, you get that wake-up call in the middle of the night because, you know, prices have gone up or one of the particular donors who have been incredibly generous to us decides to give elsewhere, and it's almost heart attack season." She added, "So far we've been blessed, and, for every downturn, we've experienced an upturn to keep us still going with strong momentum. Yet it is something that keeps me awake at night. So that fear of survival is very valid."

"Surely for everybody, not just me or you," she murmured. "I agree, I mean, not everybody has a six-month nest egg for emergencies. And, even if they did, it would probably be something that they would have to tap into, and that dwindling balance would then probably bring on the same kind of fear because now they won't have it." Lana paused, then added, "And that's just the money angle. There is also the health angle and the mind-set perspective too."

Dani laughed. "All good points. I think we're all just messed up then," she said, with a smile.

"Well, let's hope that, as time goes on, we all get a little bit *less* messed up and a little bit more secure."

"I think you have to be happy or secure knowing that

you can handle the worst that life throws at you," Dani murmured. "And you can't really get to that point, until you have some challenges."

"Oh, I do like that thought process concept too," Lana stated.

Dani nodded. "We do try to teach the patients here to get well-adjusted mentally and to be okay with the worst thing in life because then everything else becomes a whole lot easier to deal with. Not everybody likes that kind of thought process and tries to make it sound like it's a defeatist attitude. Yet we do find it helps a lot of people if they can come to terms with, you know, the worst thing, the worst outcome. And then everything else is a step up."

"Agreed." Lana frowned, deep in thought.

And, with that, she headed back to her desk and the stack of work waiting for her. It still was a job. It still was part of her life spent here, and it still was something that she wanted desperately to keep and to be a part of. And to think that so much was going on around her all the time, that she didn't necessarily have the same level of awareness about, was also interesting.

She wondered about signing up for more training, so she could do more here. At the same time, she had never really considered her survival needs at this level, but she could see how that fear was eating away at her—or had been now that it had been triggered. Plus, if Lana trained for something else, maybe Dani would have even more reasons to keep Lana on. She considered that, as she worked through the rest of the day. Finally, at 5:00 p.m., she stopped in again at Dani's office.

Dani took one look and remarked, "*Uh-uh*, that's a pretty serious look on your face."

"Well, it just goes back to what I was saying earlier, about survival. If you ever did come to the point where you needed to lay me off," she began, "I would like to stay here. So, if there was a chance to train for some other position, where you still have need for people here, then—any time that opportunity comes up—I would jump at it." And, with that said, Lana didn't even wait for Dani to respond. Lana just turned and walked back out.

RYATT WORKED HARD the next few days, more than ecstatic to see concrete results from his last session with Shane.

Even Shane commented on it. "Seems like a change of attitude has happened," he noted, with a big grin.

"Nothing like seeing progress," Ryatt agreed, pasting on his own bright smile.

"Isn't that the truth? Sounds like I should have done that earlier."

"Well, I may not have been ready to see it either. Sometimes just because we want to be ready doesn't mean we are."

Shane nodded, his gaze thoughtful as he studied Ryatt. "Lots of changes in attitude, from what I'm seeing."

Ryatt laughed. "Definitely a few, yes. And not a moment too soon," he murmured. "Wish I hadn't been quite such a jerk when I first arrived."

"Yeah, me too," Shane agreed, startling a laugh out of Ryatt.

"See? That's what I needed. Somebody to act normal, to act natural, and to not let me get away with any kind of guff or anything."

"It's not even so much about letting you get away with

it, it's realizing that you're not quite in a state where anybody can push you. It's definitely up to you to do the rehab on your own, with or without our assistance. However, if you're not ready and if you can't see that progress is happening or that you're not in a state for anybody to even talk to you, it makes your recovery more difficult."

Ryatt nodded. "I get that now. Thanks for having the perseverance to keep pushing."

"Not a problem," Shane replied, with a bright smile. "It's what I do."

"And you do it very well."

Shane looked surprised at the compliment but also pleased, and Ryatt realized just what a bear he'd been. He promised himself mentally to do better. The medical personnel especially weren't here to wait on him, and yet, in many ways, that's exactly what they had been doing, and it shouldn't need to be.

Ryatt kept working throughout the rest of the week, seeing Lana as much as he could. Yet quietly looking for a way to reach acceptance for himself and others. He was likely hardest on himself. And that wasn't something that anyone else could really help him with. Some, sure. Just not enough.

One day at lunch, he arrived, tired and worn out.

She looked at him, frowned, and asked, "Are you doing too much in Shane's sessions?"

"No," Ryatt replied immediately. "And I do want to keep pushing physically. It's just hard to know what to do in my future."

"Ah," she noted, "you're into that more mental stage."

He frowned at her. "Are there stages to this rehab process?"

"I don't know, but I imagine that there's got to be different levels, where certain things become more important. When you're here, it's … Sometimes it's just about even being able to sit up, and, at a future point in time, you see that you'll have a life after being here. Then it becomes a case of, *If I'm getting my life back, what will I do with it?*"

He laughed. "You're right, and it is something like that. It just seems kind of odd to even be looking forward, when I'm not there yet physically or even timewise. Except I know it's racing toward me."

"But you're not far off," she noted quietly. "And that's huge." And then she frowned and looked down at her plate.

"And what's that look for?" he asked, nudging her.

"I'll miss you," she said immediately.

He frowned at that. "Oh." And then he nodded. "You're right. Progress does change things, doesn't it?"

"It's not supposed to," she argued. "I mean, as much as it's good changes and it's happy changes—and that's what should be happening here. However, it also feels … I don't know. I mean, *wrong* is not the right word for it, but it feels *odd* maybe." She shrugged. "I know that's not quite right either."

"It's okay. I guess, once again, it's an adjustment."

She nodded. "That it is. … How's your sister doing?" she asked.

"She's doing great," he murmured. "Shane seems to have really helped get her pain under control, and the at-home exercises are working for her," he noted absentmindedly.

"Perfect," she said in a bright and cheerful voice.

He nodded. But her words had given him something to think about. What would he do when he left here? And how would he keep seeing her? "How do you feel about long-distance relationships?" he asked suddenly. Then, seeing the surprise on her face, he wished he'd kept his mouth shut.

"What are you talking about?"

"When I leave," he murmured.

"And where are you going when you leave?" she asked curiously. "I don't think I've ever asked where you're from. I assumed because your sister was here that you lived close by."

"I wasn't living near here," he replied. "I was in California, when I had my surgeries. But I was planning on staying near Quinton. It is just my sister and me."

"Well, in that case," she said, "it's hardly a long-distance relationship to keep seeing you around here in the Dallas area."

"I guess," he murmured, "but I also have to establish a way to make a living or some kind of a career path for myself."

"But you don't have to do it all at once," she stated firmly.

"No, no, you're right," he agreed. "Yet it does feel like maybe it's time."

"Feeling that way, is one thing, but getting worried about plans for your future, that's a whole different story."

He laughed. "I get it, and nothing is allowed to make me feel stressed, right?"

She grinned. "See? You already got this part figured out."

"No," he disagreed, "but I wish I did."

"And again," she said, with that gentle warning tone of hers, "not too much, not too fast."

"Got it," he replied. "You still didn't answer my question."

"That's because it's not long-distance if you're staying anywhere in town."

"Well, I was thinking about *town*," he stated, with a nod. "Just not exactly sure what town living will mean."

"I got that," she added. "I live in town myself anyway."

"Right," he murmured, "I had forgotten that. Do you have an apartment?"

She nodded. "That I do. I used to live with several girlfriends, and they've all pretty well moved on in various aspects of their lives, so I live alone now."

"And you like that?"

"Not particularly," she noted cheerfully, "but I'm here so much of my time that it's not really an issue."

"I hadn't even considered that. You automatically assume that life after being here will be perfect, but, of course, it'll be an adjustment."

"And adjustments are not necessarily bad either," she pointed out, as a reminder.

He smiled. "Nope, they don't have to be, do they? Even my sister's got a pretty big upcoming adjustment."

"And the wedding's coming up faster and faster."

"I'll probably still be here, particularly at the rate that I'm going."

"Hey, you've shown a ton of progress," she noted.

"Thank you," he said, a big grin on his face. "I'm still not quite ready to fly the coop just yet."

"No, of course not," she murmured. "But, just so you know, we all think you're doing fabulous."

He felt pleasure hearing her words, sharing the thoughts of others, all sprinting across his body and mind. Something that he hadn't had here—until now. "And I'm really glad to hear that. I'm kind of making up for being a cranky jerk when I first got here."

She laughed. "You know what? I think that bothers you

more than it bothers anybody else."

"It does bother me," he murmured. "It's not who I am inside."

"And maybe that's why it doesn't bother anybody," she suggested gently. "Everybody knows that that was a person in a lot of pain, recovering from major trauma, whereas now you're a very different person."

"I'm glad to hear that. To think I could still be that same person would be pretty rough."

She nodded. "I hear you there, but you've made incredible progress."

The conversation quickly turned to other things at that point, but it kept him thinking about what his plans were because he didn't really have any.

When his sister stopped by later that next day, he mentioned to her, "I'm at least starting to think about what's coming after this," he murmured. "I'm just not getting any answers."

She stared at him and then nodded. "It's not an easy thing to decide either, and we tend to think that there's only one choice and that, if we make the wrong one, it's a lifetime decision."

He looked at her, frowning. "That's exactly what I'm afraid of."

She smiled. "I'm just a little bit ahead of you on that pathway," she noted. "And I already went the wrong direction once."

"Meaning?"

"I jumped back into law," she replied, "and I'm not sure it was the right decision, but I've spent so much time and energy getting there that it feels like something I can't walk away from."

"Maybe it's time to change the type of law you do?" he asked curiously, because he'd never heard her talk like this before.

"Maybe," she agreed, "it's definitely something I'm thinking about now."

"Because of Stan or Shane?"

"Both in a way. Because of what I want out of life after this too." She flushed. "I'd really like a family," she shared. "Particularly after thinking for the longest time that I could never have one."

"Why couldn't you have a family?"

"Just think about my boss, for one," she said, with an eye roll. "And the fight I had to even get a few weeks off to recover here."

"I would say, tell them to stuff it and move on with your life, but I know it's not that easy for you."

"It isn't," she stated. "And it's definitely something I have to work my way through."

He nodded. "I agree. At the same time, I understand your earlier point. You've spent an awful lot of time getting to where you are, and it would be a shame to throw it all away."

"That's what I mean though," she explained. "It becomes something that you hang on to because it's something you accomplished, and a lot of work and money went into it, but if it's not something I'm enjoying …"

"What if it was something different, still law but, you know, different law?"

"Meaning?"

"I don't know," he admitted. "Does Dani have a lawyer on speed dial around this place? Maybe she would like one."

Quinton snorted. "I have no idea." She frowned. "It

never even occurred to me, but I'm sure she has some lawyers involved. She would have to. There's an awful lot of legal paperwork involved when running a charity, like here."

"Exactly," he said, "and I know that you and Stan spend a lot of time together, which means you are here a lot, so maybe that's something that you could look at, that you could run by Dani one day."

"Maybe," Quinton replied, staring off in the distance. "Certainly worth talking to her about."

"Exactly. And now that we've solved your problems," he quipped, "what about mine?"

She burst out laughing. "Wouldn't it be nice if it were that easy?"

He nodded. "I keep hoping, but, so far, I'm not really finding any clarity that I need."

"You will," she declared. "I promise you will. It's just got to take its own time to wrap through your head. You've always been really interested in having your own business, so that seems like something you could easily do."

"I was thinking about it," he admitted, "because again it is something I want to do, but I wasn't sure I wanted a sedentary lifestyle. I'll end up in trouble just because I can't get out and do enough to keep my body limber and moving freely. Although I was reminded, not too long ago, that contemplating a business of some kind doesn't have to be behind a desk."

Lana's earlier suggestion from one of their many discussions had merit too. If he provided supplies for hiking and outdoor activities, like camping equipment, he might be able to resurrect an old hobby—photography—and build that up, while out testing the equipment. Have an online profile where he was out taking pictures. He frowned, considering it, when he realized Quinton was still talking to him about it.

"What about a business linked to some kind of fitness program?" she suggested. "I think it's all about balance, and you and I? We tend to be all or nothing. We went into the service, and that was definitely an all-or-nothing lifestyle for us. And, when it became nothing, we were both kind of stopped in our tracks, not sure what we would do next."

He smiled. "I never would have thought that you and I were even close to being the same," he admitted, "but the more I'm here, the more I realize that we really are very similar."

She grinned. "Absolutely. And I hear that there might be somebody in your life too," she said in a teasing tone. "Does that have anything to do with the questions about your future?"

"Some," he confirmed. "I did ask how she would feel about a long-distance relationship. Yet she didn't really answer me."

"Are you leaving?" Quinton asked, an eyebrow shooting up, and he noted the dismay on her face.

"No, but whatever I do in the future, I still won't be here at Hathaway, and it seems like this is almost a village in itself."

She smiled. "Ah, so what you were really asking is whether your relationship was tied to you being here."

"I guess," he replied, startled. "I hadn't really thought about it that way."

"But that seems to be what you are asking, is it not?"

"I really want to know if she still is interested in a relationship, if I'm no longer here at Hathaway House."

"Which is what you were asking then, but probably not

making it clear enough for her."

He winced. "Yeah, it's a little hard to make things clear how you feel when you're not really sure how you feel."

"No. You know how you feel, if you asked her that question. You're probably just not sure how *she* feels. Otherwise you wouldn't have had the doubt."

He stared at her. "You know that it's not that easy."

"Don't start with me," she said, shaking her head. "I've been down the same pathway that you're going down. So I know it's not that easy, but I also know that anything worth doing is worth doing right. So, in order for you to get back on your feet and to find a life again, you need to be doing it the right way."

"And that is?" And, of course, he threw out the challenge in his voice more to get her off his back because he wasn't quite ready to go that route. Yet nuggets of gold were in this conversation that he needed to consider.

But she came back with a ready answer. "Finding out exactly what's in your heart and deciding it's worth it and going after it—whether it's Lana or a business," she noted quietly. "And not letting anybody say no or try to stop you. It's nobody else's life, and nobody else will care quite the same as you."

Long after Quinton left, Ryatt pondered her words of wisdom. He really, really liked Lana, but *like* was not necessarily anything more than that. And yet, in his heart of hearts, he knew that he was lying to himself; he just didn't quite understand *why* he was lying. And it was something he would have to get to the bottom of, before he went any further. Instinctively he knew that, yet he just didn't quite understand how he was supposed to go about doing it.

She was a special person, and the last thing he wanted to

do was upset her or get her into any kind of relationship that he wasn't prepared to carry out. He definitely needed to figure out his own mind, before he brought it up again with her. And, with that, he fell into a deep meditative state, as he pondered the relationships in his life and where he wanted them to go.

The last thing he wanted was to let her down. *Like I'd let Peter down.*

He winced at that. He'd been outsourcing supplies, when the truck they were in drove over an IED. He'd been injured but not as badly as his friends. In the shape he was in, he knew he had a chance to save one and one only. So he chose the one in the best shape to survive the trip. By the time Ryatt sent help back to Peter, he was gone. And the journey had cost Ryatt part of his leg. However, making that horrific decision had cost him so much more—an everlasting guilt and an inability to trust his own judgment.

Chapter 8

LANA DIDN'T KNOW quite what was wrong over the next few days, as Ryatt completely backed off when certain discussions about him popped up. She was happy in a sense that he was talking about his future because it was a very important stage of his development. Of course she wasn't too happy about the thought of him leaving, but at least he was thinking about the two of them having some kind of continuing relationship.

He'd really thrown her when he'd asked about a long-distance relationship because, if he was planning to go back to California or some such thing, that would have been incredibly hard for her to take. And she wasn't sure that she was up for something like that. It was much more difficult to keep a relationship alive and happy when they didn't live in the same state. And she wasn't sure that she could do that.

Neither did she really want to leave here because working at Hathaway House was incredibly fulfilling, and it was something she wanted to maintain. She was part of a team, helping people in a small way to make up for the fact she hadn't been able to help her mother or her father. The successes here made her both laugh and cry—but always with a sense of connection to the process and the people, all with a sense of how very necessary this center was. Yet, for the first time, she pondered what leaving Hathaway would mean. And even though it was not something that had been brought up, it could easily be something that she would have to face.

Was she willing to move for Ryatt? And, if she wasn't, then why was she even going down that relationship pathway with him? Because it would just be heartbreaking to have to tell him—at some point in time—that she wasn't willing to go there with him. And that would just make her feel even worse.

As Ryatt settled into his more pensive silences, she found herself doing the same.

Even on a break with Dani, her boss commented, "Are you okay?"

"Yeah." Lana shook her head, as if to stop her thoughts. "Just woolgathering."

"Somebody on your mind?" Dani asked, with an intuitive look.

"Definitely. It's hard to know what the answers are sometimes. I mean, he'll be leaving soon."

"Not soon," Dani corrected. "You've got months yet."

"Do we?" she asked in fascination. "He seems to think that his future has now become a burning issue."

"That's because, with somebody like him, *every* issue will become a burning issue," she noted, with a smile. "He takes every aspect of his life very seriously. And so, as he works his way through this, he won't let anything get in his way."

"No, you're right. He's quite dedicated to everything, isn't he?"

"He is. He is an intense personality."

Lana nodded. No warning had been present in Dani's voice. Her boss had just been stating a fact like a fact. And it was true; Ryatt was a very intense personality. He was also fascinating, and he was the only person in a very long time to have even caught Lana's attention—outside of curiosity and, in general, good feelings. There was something very special about Ryatt. "It is hard to know what to do," she repeated.

"Well, one of the biggest things," Dani noted, "would be to just relax and to see where it goes. And you'll find out soon enough if something's there."

"And if there is?"

"Then you have to work out some details," she stated. "But, if there's love and if there's enough of it, the details will be worked out because compromises are a natural part of life. Regardless of what the relationship is, there's a compromise involved. So you have to determine what the compromise is and whether it's something that you want. But, if it means keeping him, then you already know the answer."

Lana laughed. "It's such a funny thing to even think of having met anybody here," she stated, with marvel in her voice.

"Well, it is and it isn't," Dani replied. "We've had a lot of relationships start in this place, which has been lovely to see."

"I've been privy to watching a few of them develop myself, but I was always kind of, you know, detached."

"Of course, because it was somebody else's problem."

At that, Lana laughed again. "And there is nothing, absolutely nothing, like the pain of not knowing where your relationship is going or where you stand in a relationship."

"So you may want to clear some of that up, as soon as you can."

And, with that thought, Lana returned to her office. How did one clear up something like that when she didn't even know necessarily where she stood? Of course Dani was right; that was one of the hardest things.

Lana was determined to ask Ryatt about it, but, when she saw him at lunch the next day, seated at a table with no food before him, he already looked exhausted and worn out. She knew, whenever Ryatt arrived at lunch in his wheelchair, that he had just had a grueling workout session with Shane. Lana was just pleased that Ryatt had finally accepted that the wheelchair had its advantages, like a badge of courage. Yet he refused to eat in his wheelchair, moving over to one of the standard dining room chairs. Lana loved how unique his viewpoint was.

He looked at her, gave her a half smile. "I think I'll skip lunch. I'm feeling pretty rough."

"You want me to bring you something down later?" she asked, worried.

He shook his head. "No, maybe I'm just doing too much."

"Well, you're definitely pushing it, and I think you're starting to worry about it."

He looked at her, thought about it, then agreed. "You know something? You could be right. It's just hard to be sure. I feel like I'm on the precipice of a brave new world, just not so certain I'm brave enough for that new world." He gave her a mocking grin.

"You are," she said quietly. "I've never seen anybody braver."

He stared at her and then smiled. "Thank you for that." He got up slowly, obviously hurting, to shift from the dining room chair to his wheelchair. "I'll see you tomorrow?" he asked, a question to his tone.

She nodded. "Absolutely, go and rest up."

As Ryatt slowly made his way back to his room, he had to wonder even why he had this hesitation in his life. He should just do his darndest to lock up that relationship, so Lana wouldn't think him indifferent and seek another. They could work out right now whatever it was that they needed to work out to face the future together. He wasn't even sure that they needed to work out anything; he just knew that he still had a lot of stuff in his own head to deal with, and he admitted that he was no prize at the moment.

Maybe he wouldn't be a prize at the end of the day either; he didn't know. There just seemed to be so much to deal with sometimes that he couldn't quite get himself wrapped around it all. By the time he made it to his room, he was beyond exhausted, and he just collapsed onto the bed. Shane found him an hour later. Ryatt opened hazy eyes.

Shane walked in closer, frowning. "Are you okay?"

"I'm not. Although I'm not sure what's going on, but I feel pretty rough today."

"We can skip the afternoon session, if you want."

He tried to sit back up again. "No, no, no." And then he groaned and whispered, "Well maybe," and he just flopped back again.

Shane immediately took his temperature. "I think you're sick," he murmured. "You're running a bit of a fever."

Ryatt frowned at him. "I can't remember the last time I caught a cold or the flu."

"We've had a few people down with it in the center. We've been trying hard to keep it away from the patients, but it looks like you might have it."

"Well, dang." Ryatt stared at Shane. "So much for making progress."

"This is your body's way of saying, *You're doing too much*," Shane said sternly. "I planned to have a talk with you about pushing yourself. It's been pretty evident lately that you're on some kind of a mission to ensure you're the best you can be and to get out of here as fast as you can."

"Well, best as I can be, yes," he confirmed. "Not so sure about the *getting out as fast as I can* part. It seems like I don't really have any plans once I leave here anyway. So I'm more desperate to find an answer."

"Good to know, but that's not something for you to worry about yet either."

"That's easy for you to say," he stated pointedly. "You have a job. You have a career. You have a partner. An awful lot in my life is missing."

"And you'll get them, every one of them," Shane said firmly, "but not until your body is ready. What you don't want to do is collapse and be stuck here for another six months. That's not progress for anyone."

Chapter 9

L ANA HAD BEEN spending a lot of time thinking about her fears and what she would do about them, what she might possibly do to help work herself through them. It was an ongoing project. Yet somehow she felt that, once she came to a decision, a conclusion—even if the first of many later on—then she would feel an urgency to face them, to share this with Ryatt.

When Lana started work the next day, Dani stopped in later that morning and said, "By the way, I just wanted to let you know that I've added staff training in the field of fears that you were talking about. I think more of us need to have a definitive idea about what our patients here have for fears and how to properly deal with them."

"That's a good idea, and it can be applied to the staff as well." Lana nodded. "I have to admit that I was a little concerned myself. I've spent a bunch of time, even again last night, thinking about the fears that I've been harboring, without even realizing it. And especially the ones that I've allowed to rule some of my present thoughts and feelings."

Dani tilted her head. "Well, that's a good thing," she replied cautiously. "At least I hope so."

"I hope so too, in the long run," she admitted, with a wry smile. "I think all it's doing right now is making me a little more confused."

"And I think fears also tend to be something that we're raised with. They're other people's beliefs, maybe not necessarily our own. So, when you're out in the real world, you have to reexamine the things that you believe and don't believe and find out for yourself if they're really parts of who you are or if they're just bits and pieces of other people sticking to you."

Lana stared at her boss. "Wow. I've never heard it presented like that before, but it's really good that you did that."

"Ha." Dani laughed. "We'll just put that down to real-life experience."

"I don't know. You have a talent for this kind of stuff."

"No, no, nope." Dani shook her head. "That would be Dennis."

At that, Lana agreed. "He is a wizard when it comes to giving you a whole new perspective on life," she agreed, "but I think you're right too. And I hadn't really considered that, the whole distinction of *whose thoughts and beliefs am I harboring*?"

"And maybe it's time you did," she suggested, with a smile. "I know, with my own father, the Major, who you have met many times, I had to sit down and reassess what was important to me, what was important to him, and why was something important to me and was it only because it was important to him?" she murmured. "And believe me. If you aren't confused after that statement, you should be." She went off in peals of laughter, making Lana grin.

"I hear you. That was quite a mouthful. Yet I think I got the gist of what you're saying," Lana said. "I don't think most of us look at that concept though. We go from childhood to adulthood, and we never assess or even try to assess just where our beliefs come from and whether they still hold true for the people we are as adults."

"Exactly, and, although you may say that you have these fears, are they your fears, or are they fears that you've absorbed from other people?" Dani asked, warming up to a topic that she obviously cared a lot about. "Are fears of losing your job akin to fears of losing your mother? Both are foundations, main supports in our lives, and fears are easily transferred."

"I have no idea," Lana admitted in fascination. "I'll have to give that some more thought."

"Do that. You might be surprised that it's less about fear and as much as it's about uncertainty, about a change. For instance, you probably have enough money that, should you lose your job, you'd be okay for a little while. So is it really a fear that you will not have enough money, or is it an uncertainty about what you'll do next and how you'll survive? And, if you trust that you're strong enough to handle whatever comes your way, then it's not so much about a fear as it's just that specific challenge that you're not certain that you'll rise to." And, with that, she added, "And that's my phone ringing. I've got to run."

Dani dashed off to her office, leaving Lana standing here, completely bemused at the turn of events and the words of wisdom that had just been shared with her. She almost wished she had had a recorder, so that she could tape it and think about it later. A lot of nuggets were in that little speech Dani had delivered that Lana would like to hear again, over and over a few times, just to reassess what she was supposed to get out of it.

But Dani was right on a couple levels. Lana hadn't questioned whether these were fears or more about uncertainty—unmade plans. And she hadn't critically assessed whether the fears she had were even ones that were justifiably hers. Her mother had been fearful of everything; she would refuse even going out at night. As far as she was concerned, the boogeyman was out there and would get her, no matter what. And she'd had more or less raised Lana that way, even though Lana nor her mother had never been in a situation that even had engendered a physical fear. No one should be walking outside in the dark, especially in the alleyways, putting themselves in a position where they were likely to find trouble.

Putting oneself in a position where trouble was likely to find you? Now there was a big difference. As Lana pondered it more and more, she had to sit down with a pen, even though it was work hours, and write down some of the fears that she was facing. One of them, she had to stop and think about—the supposed fact that she was afraid she would always be alone. Particularly given the loss of her mother physically, and the loss of her father emotionally.

It's not that her biological clock was ticking, but, from her mother's point of view, Lana's biological clock *was* ticking, and so there was always this pressure, this fear, that *Hey, you need to get married and settle down and have a family, before it's too late.* And it was the *before it's too late* part that added so much more urgency—and, yes, fear—to that thought.

By the time Lana had worked through lunch and made it to the end of her day, she had to go to her dentist appointment. So she booked it out of the office without even talking to Ryatt. She sent him a quick text message, saying, she was gone for the day and hoped he had a good night. When she didn't get an answer back, she didn't think anything of it. After all she'd just run out herself, so, if he had other stuff to deal with, well, it was no surprise, given everything going on in his life.

But testing her fears earlier today was something that made her reconsider some of the aspects surrounding what she had taken for granted as being normal and natural fears. And something that she would have to spend a whole lot longer on in order to reprogram her mind. Thanks to Dani, Lana had a whole new perspective to explore. And it was a surprise because Dani wasn't even somebody that Lana necessarily would have thought was into this kind of introspection. Dani made it look effortless.

But, when the opportunity to test her beliefs had presented itself to Lana, she found it hard to back away. Particularly when Ryatt was doing something similar. She was dying to tell him about these new points that Dani had brought up, hoping that maybe it would help him too. Yet, even as she got in the next morning, her workload was crazy, and the phone rang off the wall. At noon, she looked up with tired eyes to find Ryatt sitting in his wheelchair at her doorway, gazing at her quizzically. She smiled with relief.

"I'm really glad you're not somebody else wanting something from me right now," she admitted, throwing down her pen, "because honestly, I'm done."

"Lunchtime?" he asked gently.

"Yes," she cried out with enthusiasm. And even then her stomach growled.

He laughed. "Come on. Let's go."

And she dropped everything, got up, and smiled at him. "Perfect timing. I so need this break," she murmured.

"Good," he said. "I wasn't sure when I got that message from you late yesterday if you're even up for lunch."

"If it's a case of not being up for lunch, it means that I

just don't have time," she explained. "Things have been really hectic recently."

"I get that. Your marketing plans mean a lot of balls in the air. Juggling is emotionally draining."

She nodded, without even thinking about it. "Yep, I sure have many aspects to handle, but that's all right. I'll get on top of all the work sooner or later."

He smiled. "No longer worried about losing your job?" he asked in a teasing tone.

"Ha, funny you should mention that because Dani said something the other day that just blew me away." As they made their way back down to the cafeteria, she explained it to him.

"Wow," he murmured in a soft voice. "Not exactly the kind of conversation you'd expect, is it?"

"No, and yet that seems like a judgment in itself," she added, with a smirk, "because Dani is definitely *very* ... I don't want to say *advanced* but ..." She shrugged. "Let me just say, she's very in tune with who she is."

"And that can be good," Ryatt replied, with a nod. "However, I wonder if too much of that's a bad thing though."

"Maybe, nobody wants to be too into this stuff that you forget the world around you is for living, not just for learning."

"If it were just about learning lessons," he added, "I'd be wondering what kind of a jerk I was in a past life to deserve this."

"And maybe what it was is life itself was just too easy for you," she offered, with a smile. "Maybe you needed to come in with a bigger challenge so that you could step up to and show how good you are with it."

He laughed at that. "Just think. Can you imagine if it was something like that?" He shook his head. "Wow."

She just smiled and stepped into the buffet line, where Dennis stood on the other side of the counter, serving up lunch.

When he got to them, he grinned. "There you are. What will it be today?"

She quickly picked out several lunch items.

"Hungry are you?" Dennis asked.

"I am, indeed," she murmured, "and I missed lunch yesterday." The look on his face had her laughing out loud. "It's not that bad," she protested.

"Missing any meal's bad," he argued, as he patted his own stomach. "My stomach will not tolerate one meal missed," he added, with a big smile.

"Yeah, but that's your tummy. Most of us have missed many a meal and not really noticed it."

"Oh, I don't know about that. I think, when you say, *most people*, I think you mean yourself."

She chuckled and moved ahead and grabbed a cup of coffee and some water. As she waited for Ryatt to come in behind her, she realized his tray was overfull, and he was on crutches today.

Immediately she said, "Let me put this down, and I'll come right back." She raced over, found an empty table, left her tray, and then came back to help Ryatt.

He looked at her, with a mock grin. "One of these days I'll do this without help. Although it will probably be when I'm in the wheelchair or finally on my prosthetic."

"Hey," she said, "that day's ahead of you, but it doesn't have to be today."

"You guys are all just way too understanding and helpful. In the previous place where I was, people would laugh to see me fall and wipe out."

"That would just make me very sad."

"People are people," Ryatt said. "Some came from the heart, and some just from viciousness because they were happy it wasn't them in our situation."

"Still no excuse for it," she stated stoutly.

He grinned. "And that's why you're a nice person, and those others weren't."

She shrugged. "Life's too short to not be nice," she murmured. "It's a hard enough thing for each of us to get along in this world," she explained. "So doing it *and* helping somebody else get along a little easier should give us brownie points."

"Unless," Ryatt pointed out, "you're doing it *just* for the brownie points, and then, of course, you don't get brownie points at all."

At that, she started to laugh. "Unfortunately I think you're quite right there too."

LUNCH WAS A jovial affair, and Ryatt was happy to see Lana back in a good mood. She'd seemed almost too introspective and sad a few days ago, and he'd worried that some of this stuff was getting to her. But today she seemed to be back to normal, if a little too busy and chaotic in her world. "Are you dealing with those fears that you were talking about the other day?" he asked her, when she'd finished eating.

She looked up, shrugged. "I might *think* that I am. I'm not sure that I'm succeeding though."

He nodded. "Isn't that the truth? We do the best you

can, but that doesn't necessarily mean that we're accomplishing what we think we need to. And I'm not sure we ever have the answer to it either. At what point in time are we supposed to just acknowledge that life is a challenge, and we should do the best we can and keep moving?"

She nodded. "I hear you there," she murmured. "Sometimes we should just let it be as is, maybe let something else take the number one slot. I think sometimes you need to take a closer look, and then the trick really is to know when to do one or the other. And not to get hung up on it, to not forget to enjoy life and those around you," she murmured, as she took a sip of her coffee. "When you think about it, as soon as you deal with one issue, another one'll come along anyway."

"So does that mean we don't even bother starting?" he teased, with a big grin.

"Maybe," she admitted, "at least sometime, when it seems so hard, *not bothering* would be an easy answer, right?"

"An easy answer maybe," he agreed, "but, in my case, I'm supposed to do a lot of that kind of introspection here—almost as homework—so easy answers won't get me anywhere. You can bet that I've still got that whole team behind me, waiting for me to show progress."

"Showing progress is one thing though," she noted. "Being forced to feel like you must progress or you don't get to stay, that's a whole different story. And we will start doing some staff training in that area, particularly to help with the patients' fears in that regard."

He stared at her, nodding. "You know what? That's probably a good idea."

"I think so. I did bring it up with Dani, and she likes the idea of doing more along that line."

"Good," he said. "I think it's a mistake for anybody to get a little too complacent about who and what they are in life, especially if you don't start to see what's going on around you."

"And yet, in a place like this, I think we're all just so busy," she added quietly, "and every day happens so fast and goes by before you've had a chance to even register it's over. Then you're on to the next day and all new problems."

"I get that," Ryatt replied. "And the patient rotation must also change constantly, so that the staff are always looking at new problems, new issues, and new people. That kind of training is something that has to be introduced right from the beginning, when each new patient arrives," he murmured.

"I was thinking of that," she noted. "It should be just almost like one of the golden rules when you arrive—what to expect, what not to expect, how to handle disappointment, and what to do when you're starting to worry about your progress or lack of progress."

He nodded. "And that doesn't necessarily have to be laid out quite so clearly in black-and-white but at least have people know that they can freely ask questions, that they have options."

She smiled. "And, in your case, good options."

"I hope so," he said. "I'm feeling like I'm working hard and getting back some of what I put into it."

"I think that's really a great stage to reach," she shared, "especially after all those times where you put in the work and didn't see the benefits yet."

He nodded in agreement, looked over at her, and asked, "Did you ever realize just how much in tune we are with each other?"

She snorted. "I was thinking about that earlier," she said.

"And," he asked teasingly, "any decisions?"

"No, not at all." She laughed. Then she hesitated and added, "Sometimes I wonder if we aren't too close."

He stopped, stared at her in surprise, a questioning look in his eyes. "Is that a problem?"

"Only if we're both missing the same point. Otherwise I don't think so," she replied, "but I haven't really figured it out."

"Well, maybe this is just one of those things that you don't need to figure out, but maybe just accept."

She smiled and nodded. "That probably works too."

"*TOO CLOSE,*" RYATT muttered to himself and worried over that concept for several days. He didn't say anything to her, but he wondered. When his sister showed up a few days later, he looked at her, smiled, and asked, "How are you doing?"

"I'm doing fine," she said. "I came by to see how you were doing though."

He shrugged. "I'm okay."

"And yet you seem a little preoccupied. What's going on?"

He laughed. "Just because you're my big sister doesn't mean I tell you everything."

"You always used to," she noted in a cajoling voice. "Don't you remember?"

"Sure, but I was ... what? All of five?"

She burst out laughing. "Maybe. However, sometimes it's just nice to talk to somebody."

He shrugged. "Just something somebody said that I'm not sure how to take."

"Like what?"

He frowned, hesitated, and then figured, why not share? "Well, what the heck." And he mentioned what Lana had told him.

"*Too much alike*," Quinton repeated thoughtfully, staring off in the distance. "Well, I guess that can be considered in two ways. One, that's a good thing—in the sense that you're very compatible, that you understand each other, and, because your thoughts would be very similar to each other, your way of thinking would be similar to each other, maybe almost like being old friends, yet in a short amount of time."

He nodded. "I was thinking along that line, but I'm not so sure."

"Well, the other way to look at it would be that there's no spark, there's no excitement, because you already know each other so well," she suggested. "So I guess it depends on how you feel about it. Do you think that you're already past that stage of getting to know each other so that you already are at the *comfortable like an old shoe* type of relationship?"

He shook his head. "I don't think so. I just … It was an odd thing for her to say."

"But it seems like you've had a lot of conversations with her, where you're on the same side of the *getting to know each other* mat, and maybe that's all that she means."

"Maybe." Ryatt frowned. "It just made me a little …" And then he didn't know what to say. "I don't … I don't know. It's foolish, and, no matter what I say at this point in time, it makes me look like an idiot."

She burst out laughing. "That is something you're not and never have been."

"Maybe not," he agreed, "but I'm also still struggling with my future and what I want to do when I get out of here."

"Well, pick wisely," she said, and then she stopped and shook her head. "No. Forget that. Do what you can now, and, if you need to change it down the road, do so. The question for you on that earlier issue is, how do you feel about her in your heart? Does she feel like somebody you want to have close all the time, or does she feel like an old friend you'd like to visit with but, you know it's okay when she leaves again?"

He winced at that. "That doesn't sound very romantic."

"There's a lot to be said for romance, and there's an awful lot more to be said for love."

"Is there a difference?"

"Absolutely. One is the start, and the second is the finish," she explained, "as long as you understand that you're both good to go. Personally I think there's an awful lot to be said about having a partner who's a very good friend to the point that you can finish each other's sentences, that you have the same beliefs on each topic, so no arguments really," she murmured. "I know a lot of people like to have relationships that are full of much more conflict. Somehow the conflict helps them keep their relationship alive, and that's the way they want it. For me, that's not what I want," she declared. "I feel like all my military experience was enough conflict. I want peace now and to know that peace is possible, so I don't live in another war zone, whether physically or emotionally. For some it's the spice, and it's the excitement. They want lively discussions and hard arguments. But I want to express my point of view and not have it argued. Debated? Yes, that's fine, but I really don't want that level of conflict anymore."

"No," Ryatt murmured. "I get it." And long after Quinton was gone, he realized just how much he did get. Because Quinton was right. They had spent a lot of time in war-torn countries, dealing with some unimaginable horrors, and that was the last thing that he wanted in his personal life too.

SEVERAL DAYS LATER Ryatt sat quietly by the pool, when Lana popped up beside him.

"Hey," she said. "I was just walking down to Stan's. What are you up to?"

"I just finished a workout in the pool," he replied, "so *resting,* I guess is the better answer. I need to go up and get a shower and get changed, but that's a long way away at the moment."

She nodded, and her gaze was a little concerned but not too bad.

At least not enough that he felt that any pity was in it. "I'm fine." He gave a wave of his hand.

"Good. Yet it was almost instinctive that I come here. So, when I saw you, I came running."

"I'm fine," he repeated, with a smile. "And it's all good."

"It just goes along with what I was saying about how we seem to know each other so well."

"Well, we do and we don't," he stated, "and I'm okay with that. My sister pointed out how she spent an awful lot of time in war-torn countries—and I did too—dealing with strife and conflict, and I'm really good to not have any more of that in my world."

"Oh, I understand that," she agreed warmly. "And I

guess then it's a good thing that we understand each other. So it's not as if we're expecting anything different."

"I guess it depends on whether you're looking for fireworks," he added quietly, "or if you're looking for two people to sit on rocking chairs on a deck, holding hands as the years go by—peaceful, happy, content, challenging each other to grow and yet not overly worried about it being a competition."

Her eyes glistened, as with tears. She nodded. "Now that sounds lovely."

Just then she got a call from someone up on the deck of the dining room. "Oops, and there's my call again." She squeezed his fingers. "You look after yourself," she murmured. "I'd hate if anything happened to you." And, with that, she was gone.

Chapter 10

L ANA KEPT WORKING through the rest of her workweek, her mind buzzing with thoughts and conflict and worries. Finally, toward the end of the day, she stopped in at Dani's office. "You got a moment?"

Dani looked up and nodded. "Have a seat."

Lana closed the door and frowned at Dani's questioning look. "I just don't want to be overheard," she murmured.

"Problems?"

"Yes and no. And I'm not sure where I'm going with this."

"So we're talking about your love life, and we're talking about Ryatt."

"Everybody knows, don't they?"

"Everybody can see the way the wind's blowing," Dani said cautiously, "but nobody can assume anything. That's your life, your relationship. And I don't know how serious you are."

"Well, that's the thing," she said. "I thought we were serious. Then I thought we weren't serious. I wasn't trying to push him. I was trying to back off and to give him space. And he mentioned something, and then I responded with something, and, instead of getting clarity, I think we're getting more confused."

"Wow, all of that, huh?"

"Right? I know. It doesn't make any sense because really I should just sit down and talk to him about it. And, if I can't sit down and talk to him about it, then it doesn't say much for whatever relationship we do or do not have," she murmured.

"Yes, but the path to that final destination is not always the easiest. He seems to be doing really well, as far as working through problems." Dani nodded.

"And I would agree with that. And he's brought up several other really important issues." And she mentioned what he'd said about growing old together.

"That is the epitome of an ideal long-term marriage," Dani offered, with a smile. "Is that not what you also want?"

"I do," she said, "but I also want to know that the person I choose cares about me more than anything," she admitted, "and then I feel totally selfish about that."

"Selfish?" Dani stared at her. "Why on earth would you feel selfish?"

"I don't know. Maybe because it just seems like it's a selfish thing to want."

"You want to be loved. And you want that to be a true love. So, other than that, is there anything else that matters?"

"I don't think so." And then Lana shrugged. "Yet it just seems like we talk about personal growth. We talk about being so close that we're almost two peas in a pod. I think that sounds like a good thing, and then he makes a comment that makes me think that he thinks it's *not* a good thing. So then I make a comment back, which I thought was trying to make it sound like a good thing again."

At that, Dani held up her hand. "Stop," she said, laughing. "I think you're both on the same side of the same argument," she said gently. "You just need time to figure out how you each feel."

"I don't want him to think that I'm not interested, but I'm really trying not to push him because I want him to be sure. And he's the one who's got so many decisions to make. And he wants such a different life in front of him now that I don't want him to think that he has to settle for something less."

"And are *you* something less?" Dani asked, staring at her in fascination.

Lana blushed. "I know that doesn't sound very good when I speak of myself as less than. And I didn't mean it the way it came off."

"That's a good thing," Dani noted. "Otherwise we'd be having a completely different talk right now."

Lana smiled at that. "I know. It's all confusing to me. I just didn't want … I wanted him to know that I was a friend."

"Ouch." Dani winced.

"What do you mean, *ouch*?"

"You friend-zoned him."

"I don't even know what that means," Lana exclaimed, with a wave of her hand.

"It means that, instead of it being in a relationship, you wanted a friend."

"I was just trying to explain to him that we were super close, in the sense that we always seem to know what the other was thinking, how we're always on the same side of every issue," she explained. "It's like … It's almost as if we're *too* much the same."

"Ouch again," Dani repeated, laughing. "That doesn't sound quite like how you may have wanted him to receive it."

"I don't know what I wanted," she murmured. "I thought I was trying to give him some options."

"*Options*," Dani said in fascination.

Lana's shoulders slumped, and she stared at her boss glumly. "I made a mess of it, didn't I?"

"I'm not even sure what *it* is," Dani admitted. "If you like the guy, tell him. If you don't like the guy, let him off the hook gently because this seems like a less painful way than whatever you're trying to do."

"In other words, sort out what I want and then tell him and be clear."

"Thank you." Dani said, with a bright smile. "Was that really that hard?"

"I didn't think so," Lana murmured, "but apparently I confused myself to no end."

"Yep, you sure did." Dani shook her head, even while smiling. "But the good news is, he's still here. He's still available. He's still around the corner, and you can still talk to him."

"And what do I say?"

"How about, *Hey, just for clarity, I really like you*," Dani suggested. "Or, even better, *I'm not sure how or when, but I've fallen in love with you …*"

"Well, I can hardly do that," Lana protested.

"Why? Because you'd be the one to speak up first?"

She flushed at that. "Right, we're back to that old fear again, aren't we?"

"I don't know," Dani said. "Are you? And then what fear is that?" Dani asked. "Fear of not being liked? Fear of not being good enough? There are all kinds of fears. Maybe you should sort out what it is you really want from him and then, instead of giving him mixed messages, come right out and be honest about it."

"Well, it all sounds good in theory."

"It also sounds good in practice too," Dani declared. "You just have to share your thoughts better and let him know. Both of you. He's the one with the biggest worries. He's the one who's not whole physically. He's the one who has and will have long-term medical issues. He's the one who'll have to retrain for a new career. All kinds of stuff are ahead of him that are not guaranteed in any way at all. So, if he has some insecurities, I get it—particularly when it comes to relationships. What you need to look at is what *you* need, so that you're clear on that, and then you need to tell him. Don't keep boxing around, playing games. That's not what he needs right now."

"Got it," Lana said. She took a deep breath. "The thing is, I already know what I want."

"What's that?"

"I want him. I just don't think he's ready at all for a committed relationship."

"And are you?" Dani asked in a very serious tone. "You're the one who's brought up all kinds of different stuff here lately. Maybe you need to bring up more stuff. Maybe you're not ready either."

Trouble was, Lana had to admit, maybe Dani was right. Maybe Lana wasn't ready at all. She wanted to be ready. She hoped she was ready, but, until it happened, was she? Maybe not.

RYATT STARED AT the shrink in front of him. "Sorry?"

"Your fears?" Dr. Sullivan asked quietly. "I mentioned

last time I wanted to assess where your fears were at."

He frowned. "Well, I thought I was doing okay with them," he murmured. "But, of course, I'm sure you'll say I'm not."

She smiled gently. "You might be surprised. We don't expect you to deal with all of them, but the most prevalent ones, if they rear their ugly heads, they do have a habit of slowing your overall progress."

Ryatt nodded. "That makes sense. *So what am I afraid of?*" he repeated, staring at the room. "Honestly, not healing enough to be independent."

She looked at him. "Is there any doubt of that happening?"

"Well, there always is," Ryatt stated. "My sister's a case in point."

"Just because your sister came back for further treatment doesn't mean that she wasn't independent and doing well on her own, before her need for more rehab."

"And she was," he conceded. "At the same time, I don't want to return to Hathaway House. I see that as a setback and maybe not in her best ..." He stopped, not even sure what he wanted to say. "I guess I just feel like, in a way, it's a failure."

"Ouch, hopefully you didn't let her know that."

"I guess it's a criticism, isn't it? I wouldn't want her to think that."

"So why do you think it's a failure?"

"Well, I just ... I guess I feel like, if it had been done properly, right from the beginning, she wouldn't have had to come back."

"That is definitely a judgment," she murmured. "And I get that. From your perspective, you probably think that you would have done better."

"And that just makes me sound like a jerk too," he said, frowning. "And I don't mean it that way."

"Well, it's interesting that that's how you view it. I think our innermost fears and views are those things that we keep inside and that we accept as normal and natural, but really they aren't necessarily so."

"I guess," he said. "I hadn't really thought about it."

"Well, let's sideline that conversation and return to why you feel like your sister's a failure."

He protested. "I'm not saying she's a failure, but …" He stopped, frowned. "Maybe I am. No, I think I'm saying that I'm afraid that her treatment was a failure. Or failed her."

"And that is a big difference there too," she noted, with a nod of her head. "But not enough of a big difference to bypass this right now."

He groaned. "Of course not. You'll make me dig into this, won't you?"

"Well, it's interesting because we don't want you to feel like you're not getting some successful treatment here. So, by thinking that your sister had a failure in her previous program, I can see how that fear would then translate into how your current program will also fail."

He stared at her. "I didn't even think of it that way."

"Well, you did because you just said so. But what I think you mean is that you didn't consciously think of it that way. It's something that's been rolling around in the back of your head in the shadows."

"I guess," he muttered. "And that's definitely not something I would want to think because, you know …" He shrugged. "I wouldn't want to even have that in my head. I don't want that to even be a possibility."

"Good," she said, with a bright smile. "So we should keep that one on the books and see how you handle it."

"What do you mean?"

"I want you to think about it, think about in what way you feel you can avoid that same scenario and not have what happened to her then happen to you."

"Well, I had thought it was a failure in her initial program," he said quietly, "but I'm now wondering if maybe it was her inability to keep up the home exercises afterward."

"Maybe. So what can you do about that?"

"I don't know," he admitted, frowning. "Maybe ask Shane for a program that's a little more manageable after I leave."

"That's one option," she confirmed, with a nod. "That's a good option too. I think they'll also be doing an outpatient program over a longer term, so people like you and your sister can come in every couple weeks for a tune-up."

He stared at her in surprise. "That would be a really good idea," he murmured. "I'd sign up for that for sure."

"And so that would also help alleviate the fear too, right?"

He frowned and nodded. "Considering I hadn't even seen it as a fear."

"No, not consciously."

He nodded. "It all comes back to that conscious versus subconscious thing again."

"Of course," she said, with a laugh. "The things that our brains can dream up ..."

"Of course." He sighed. "And I don't think my sister's a failure," he stated, a little more robustly than he had before. "It really bothers me that that even came up."

"Good, I'm glad you don't see her that way because obviously she probably wouldn't like to know that that's how you view her."

"And I don't," he protested. "I don't even know where that came from."

"Your subconscious again," she noted. "And sometimes, by viewing other people as failures, you think that something like that *can't* happen to you because you're not a failure."

"In my case," he corrected her, "I'm *more* likely to think it would happen to me because I *do* consider myself a failure." And then he stopped, frowned, and asked, "I didn't just say that, right?"

"Oh, you did," she declared very, very gently. "You absolutely did."

He groaned. "I don't think of myself as a failure."

"So why did you say that?"

He shook his head. "I have no idea. I really don't see myself as a failure. I guess I would consider that, if a relapse happened to me, then I would be a failure, which is almost as bad but not quite the same. I'm trying not to blame myself for things I couldn't control. Like Peter's death." As they'd talked at length on this issue before, he was more comfortable bringing it up again. He didn't want to blame his sister any more than he wanted to blame himself.

"So you don't see yourself as a failure right now, but you might if your program wouldn't work because you wouldn't blame the program. Instead you would blame yourself. Whereas in your sister's case, you're blaming her and the program."

He frowned. "It sounds like you've twisted up all my words, and yet I'm not sure you have."

"Nope, I'm not sure I have either," she replied, but now she was grinning.

"You like this, don't you?"

"I love seeing people come up with an understanding of who they are on the inside," she said gently. "It's important in understanding those aspects of who you are in order to let them go and to improve, to become somebody else."

"And is it possible to let it go and to become somebody else? A better version of myself?" he asked. "Because I really don't like what I'm seeing—hearing—right now."

"Good," she said immediately. "That sounds like a good thing to me."

"Maybe," he murmured. "I just don't know how to let it go."

"Well, first off, you have to stop judging your sister for being who she is."

He winced at that. "God that sounds awful," he murmured to himself.

"And I'm sure she would agree with you."

"I really love her, you know?"

"Good," she replied gently. "And I don't doubt that. Don't get me wrong. Just because you have these thoughts in your head doesn't mean that you don't care for this person, but it's your way of separating what happened to her and what is happening to you and then how you would handle it, should it happen to you."

It was convoluted, but he really did get it. And the fact that he did get it scared him even more. "I sound like a jerk," he said immediately.

She burst out laughing. "Nope, not at all, just a human being, somebody who's trying to work his way through this preamble to get somewhere specific. To not fail. To not have yet another reason to blame yourself for not being good enough."

He shook his head. "It's amazing that all this is even inside my brain," he stated. "I didn't think I was that much of a mess."

"I don't know that you're a mess at all," she declared gently. "And the fact that you're looking at this means that you're not as much of a mess as you might have been afraid you were."

"Because I'm looking at it?" he asked her.

She nodded. "The real mess is when we don't look at it, and it all just churns up on the inside and becomes this nightmare that you don't really want to deal with."

He nodded. "I get that, and you've certainly given me a lot to think about."

"Good." She nodded. "And now here's another one, a big one. If it does happen and if you do have a setback, what's the worst thing that can happen?"

"The worst thing that can happen?" He shrugged. "I'd slide backward and would have to come back here full-time."

"And then what?" she asked curiously. "Would you consider that a failure?"

He frowned. "Probably, ... but the only other option would be to buckle down and to get the job done right."

"So, if you don't do the job right, it's likely to happen? However, if you buckle in and do the job right, you're likely to avoid a relapse?"

"That makes sense, yes."

"So then your answer for right now, as to what to do to avoid this supposed failure?"

"Buckle up and make sure it doesn't happen. I never had any intention of doing anything other than that."

"I know you didn't," she said. "It's just a matter of making sure our intentions are clear and free of judgment, and you understand what you're doing and why you're doing it."

He smiled. "And to make sure that I'm not doing it for the wrong reasons, like for somebody else."

"Exactly. And who else would you do it for?" she asked, tilting her head and staring at him.

He shook his head. "Oh no, you don't. I'm not talking about my love life."

At that, she burst out laughing in delight. "Ah, but there *is* a love life, isn't there?"

He flushed. "Maybe."

"Maybe?"

"She's going through some of her own stuff right now," he murmured. "And sometimes I think … well, *she* thinks that maybe we're too close and that we're more friends than anything else."

"Well, you're friends unless you choose to delve deeper and to become something more," she explained. "You want to be on a level within a relationship where you both agree on a lot in life. At one point in time all the mystery will be gone because you'll know each other so, so well. Yet, at the same time, you also want somebody who you know will be there when you get old and gray and when you have a setback in life. Someone who knows you so well to understand that the setback is temporary and that you'll get back on your feet as soon as you can. That you'll adapt and do the best that you can with whatever life throws at you," she added. "There are different levels of knowing. I don't think anybody who's met each other for as short a time period as you have"—giving him some inclination that she already knew about the relationship—"would already know each other so well that there isn't any room for growth."

"No, you're right," he replied quietly, "but it's more

about convincing her of that."

She grinned. "Well, I have faith in you. I absolutely know that you can do this."

"But is it right if I have to do this?"

"Meaning, if you have to work at it? All things are work. Look at how much you have to dedicate yourself to your recovery here. Is a relationship any less work?" she asked him gently.

"No, I don't think so. Maybe," he said, still confused. "Now you just twisted me all up again."

"I'm not trying to," she replied, "but, if it's something worth doing—just like being here and doing the rehab right, so you don't have to come back again—then also a relationship is worth doing right too."

"But I feel like it should be right, just from the beginning."

"Which is an interesting attitude. Without even thinking about it, when I ask you a question, just give me a number rating. On a scale of one to ten, how much do you like her?"

Immediately he said, "Thirteen."

She grinned. "On a scale of one to ten, how much would you like to have her beside you when you're old and gray?"

"Fifteen," he replied immediately, his voice getting softer.

"And how about when you're both sitting on your rocking chairs, looking out over the years of your lives, having entwined them together, how much do you want her to be that person who's sitting there, having been with you through the thick and thin of everything that life's thrown at you?"

"One hundred percent," he rasped.

"So tell me," she murmured, "what's the problem?"

He looked at her in surprise. "Is it that simple?"

"Why would you make it complex?" she asked gently. "Your heart already knows what it wants. … Your mind is struggling to give it permission. The question you have to look at is why."

"I have no idea," he said, bewildered. "That makes no sense that it would."

"Sure, because it's fear."

He winced at that. "Fear again, huh?"

She laughed. "Yes, fear is great at causing all kinds of things to twist up on the inside of us and to make a mess of things."

"And how do I get rid of that fear?"

"What's the worst thing that can happen to you in regard to her?"

"She turns me down," he whispered, feeling his gut twist and realizing that the doc was right. It was fear. "Or that she isn't necessarily 100 percent on board with her and me."

"Of course she isn't because you aren't. And she can sense that. All women can, and so can men. I mean, the minute you change your attitude, you'll see an immediate reaction in hers. She'll still have her own fears to deal with," she murmured, "but they will be her fears, and you'll help allay those. Whereas you're the one who has to allay your own."

"Right. Now that you've given me a ton to think about, I think I'll go crash. My brain's on overload."

She smiled. "Maybe, but I have faith in you," she said. "You want something really badly out of life right now. And I know that it's a good thing for you. So I have faith that you'll get there." And, with that, she waved him to the door. "Go on," she said. "Rest. Relax. We'll talk again."

Chapter 11

LANA CONTINUED TO spend the next few days doing some deep thinking, getting up her resolve to tell Ryatt how much she liked him. Just so much was going on right now in her life—with Ryatt, with confronting her fears, and with this place being so busy. At one point in time, she had jokingly asked Dani if she needed to hire more staff.

Dani smiled and then nodded. "I do. I'm working on it, but it's hard to find the person with the right fit as well as the skills needed to do this job. We're a family here," she murmured. "And so I need to find the right people."

"Oh, I get it," Lana agreed. "And you're right. Hathaway House is a family, and the people here trust us, and they trust us to bring on the right people to work with them."

"You don't realize just how many different kinds of people there are until you work in a place like this. And how different everybody's point of view and their mind-set, their beliefs, all are. And how their beliefs affect their work. I mean, it just goes on and on," Dani explained. "And, most of the time, I do pretty well in choosing some really great people to have on board, but, at the moment, I'm running a little thin on a starting pool of the right people to consider hiring."

"I hear you there," Lana murmured. "And, of course, then there's the training to make sure that, regardless of the viewpoint, they still toe the company line."

At that, Dani laughed. "Isn't that the truth? And I have to admit. A few times where we had trouble with staff was with people who just didn't have the same heartwarming empathy that we needed them to have and to share with the patients. That's when I know I've rushed my hiring process. So I don't do that anymore. It's not worth it. And it's also hard for me to lay off people and to explain to them how they were not a good fit."

"I can imagine," Lana murmured. "You also come from the heart, so telling people a truth they don't want to hear has to be rough."

"It is," she agreed, "but sometimes people leave for reasons that you didn't even see coming. I had one nurse who left because she couldn't handle all the injuries. It just broke her heart every time she saw somebody. She couldn't see the good in what we were doing here at Hathaway. Instead all she saw were the broken people who arrived and not the heartwarming heroes who left. I'm sad for her," Dani said quietly. "It's got to be tough on her because she's always looking on the negative side of life. And thankfully you're always on the positive side of life," Dani said, with a smile. "Although you seem to be a little more depressed lately."

"Well, not depressed," Lana stated, "not even melancholic, maybe more contemplative."

"Ah, and that means relationship questions again."

She rolled her eyes at Dani. "No, not always," she said in protest.

"Almost always," Dani replied, "and, in your case, definitely. It's Ryatt, isn't it?"

"Maybe," she admitted. "I mean, he talks a lot now about getting his future together and what he'll do and, you know, dealing with life after being here."

"Which is all positive," she murmured. "And you still have a job, but, if you need to leave, as much as I'll be heartbroken, I will understand."

"And I wouldn't want to leave," she told Dani, "but I'm not sure how I could even possibly stay around, depending on what his plans are."

"But why worry about it until you know what his plans are?" Dani noted. "And maybe he'll surprise you. Maybe he'll stay in town."

"That would be nice," she murmured. "I would really like that."

"And it's a testament to you that you want to continue working here," Dani remarked quietly. "And people like you, ones who come from the heart? We always need more of them here."

"And maybe that's what I need to tell him too," she noted. "It does feel like home for me here."

"And that's good because we need you to feel like home because then you will stay here." Dani laughed. "Our hearts will be broken if you decide to leave."

"Well, it's not what I'm planning on doing. I don't even know that leaving is part of the options," she said, "because I'll only leave if I can't find a way to convince him to stay. And I don't even know that we're there yet."

"Listen to you," Dani noted quietly. She leaned over and gave her friend a hug. "You're already talking about your future with him down the road and how to make it work. You're all but married in your mind already."

"And is that wrong?" she asked anxiously. "I feel like I'm jumping the gun."

"No, because your heart's already happy and settled, so

it's just waiting for you to get your act together and to line everything up for it."

Lana burst out laughing. "You know what? I kind of understand what you're saying. It's just so … you know most people don't talk like that."

"Isn't that too bad," Dani murmured. "I think there's a lot of room in the world for real discussions to happen."

"I just need to talk to him some more," Lana murmured.

Dani laughed. "You absolutely do need to talk to him some more," she agreed, with a gentle smile. "Just make sure that the discussion is honest and doesn't upset him."

Lana winced at that. "Of course that ends up being the bottom line, doesn't it?"

"Now we care about you too, but our patients are here to heal and to learn how to deal with their problems and their setbacks," Dani explained. "I'm not sure another setback for him is necessarily something that we're ready for. He was a slow starter and already had some issues to deal with, so we don't want to push it."

"No, of course not."

And Dani's words kept Lana from bringing up the subject with Ryatt.

Finally he approached her and asked, "Can we talk?"

"Sure," she said. "You want to go for a walk or …?"

"Or I would like to go to the pool," he stated, "but I haven't seen you there."

"I don't live on the grounds," she explained, "so I tend not to use the amenities like that."

He nodded. "That makes sense. I hadn't thought about that."

"That's fine," she replied. "We can go sit down there. If you want to go in the pool, I would just watch."

He shook his head immediately. "No, that's no fun."

"And it's no problem either," she stated, smiling at him. "Honest." He hesitated. But she could see he really wanted to go. "Go get changed. I'll pick up coffee and bring it down for both of us."

He grinned at that. "Sounds good."

"And, hey, if we find Dennis, we might snag some ice cream."

His eyes rounded. "Sounds decadent. You know what? A few days ago I saw somebody wandering around with a big cone," he said, holding up his hands to visualize it.

She laughed. "Yes, I saw them too. I don't know who scored them though, and I don't know who was supposed to get them, but, boy, they were pretty decent looking. So I'll see what I can find."

He grinned. "Okay, I'll meet you down there in ten."

As she was done with work and had nothing to go home to, she was more than happy to stay behind and to visit with him some more. Particularly if something was on his mind. She hoped it was about them, but there was no guarantee. With Dani's words in the back of her mind always, Lana was hesitant to bring up anything that might upset him. Because Dani, of course, was right. Ryatt was here to heal, and Lana wanted to be a part of the healing process, not part of any problem.

As she walked into the cafeteria, Dennis turned toward her. "You're working late."

"I'm staying late to visit with Ryatt. He's getting changed to go into the pool."

"Are you going in with him?"

"No, I don't have a suit here, and it's not something I generally would even think about doing," she murmured.

"You know how, when you don't live on the property, it's kind of odd."

"Only odd in the sense that you leave immediately, so it feels like it's not your space."

She laughed. "That's as good an explanation as any," she murmured. "And I told him that I'd pick up coffee for us."

"Well, there's lots of that around." He motioned over to the side table.

"Ryatt also mentioned," she added, easily using him as an excuse, "that he saw some really big ice cream cones around here the other day."

At that, Dennis gave her a bland look. "Did he now? And I suppose he wants one, *huh*?"

"He does, and so do I." She grinned. "But I get it, if it's not allowed."

Dennis shrugged. "If it makes you happy, it's allowed," he said, with a smile. "And, as long as he has no food restrictions—which, as far as I know, there aren't any to do with ice cream—he's good to go." He stopped at the double doors to the kitchen and asked, "What flavor do you want and how big?"

She winced at that. "Only one scoop for me. Surprise me with the flavor," she said hurriedly. "But, for him, I don't know. Your best guess is as good as mine."

"Good enough," Dennis replied. "I'll see what I can come up with."

And, while she poured two coffees, she realized this trip would be more of a handful if she also got ice cream cones. She was still standing here, wondering if she should grab a tray, when Dennis came out, carrying one normal-size cone with probably vanilla ice cream and one monster cone with a whole lot more ice cream flavors in it.

"Wow." She stared at the cones. "That's pretty magnificent."

"Well, I chose the ice cream, so he has tiger-tiger, chocolate, and buttered rum."

"Wow," she muttered again. "What is tiger-tiger?"

"Orange and licorice."

She shuddered. "In the same bite?"

He grinned evilly. "Absolutely. You want ice cream, so I get to choose the flavors. That's the deal."

"And mine? What is mine?"

"Yours is French vanilla."

She sighed with relief. "I can get behind that one."

He laughed, and then he looked at the coffee in her hands. "Now what will you do?"

"I was thinking that maybe we could put the cones in a glass, and I could carry a tray down."

He shook his head. "How about I just come with you, and that should do the job." And, with that decided, they walked outside and down to the pool area. As she got there, Ryatt was already in the water.

He splashed up out of the water and saw her. "Hey," he said, and then he noted Dennis with the ice cream, and Ryatt's face lit up. "Wow, am I ever glad I mentioned that."

"Absolutely," Dennis agreed. "Anytime you want something, don't worry. I've got you covered." He handed over the large cone and added, "If you make a mess in the pool though, I'm not responsible."

Ryatt nodded. "I'll just sit here on the steps, if that's okay."

Dennis shrugged. "I honestly don't know what the pool rules are, but I'll get in trouble if you make a mess, and I'm really not into that, so take it easy."

"Okay, will do."

And, with that, Dennis disappeared.

Ryatt looked over at her. "Not sure what arm you had to twist," he noted, "but wow. I sent the right person after the job."

"I think he only gave it to me because it was for you," she said, grinning. "And I used your name shamelessly."

He burst out laughing. "Hey, whatever works."

"That's what I thought," she agreed, as she licked her cone.

"I have no idea what these varieties are though," Ryatt said.

"Well, that's one of the caveats Dennis mentioned. If you want a cone, you have to let him pick the flavors."

"He's fine. He's done just fine. This black one though— I mean, I absolutely adore licorice but wow. I've never had it in an ice cream before."

She looked at it and frowned. "It looks disgusting."

He grinned. "It's not. It's absolutely delicious." In companionable silence the two of them sat here, enjoying their treat.

When she finally finished hers, she got up and grabbed a napkin to wipe down her face and then said, "That was delicious. What a great idea."

"Yep," Ryatt said, "stick with me, kid, and you'll go far."

And if ever there was a segue into what she wanted to talk to him about, that was it. She hesitated and then asked quietly, "And what if that is what I want to do?"

He looked up at her, frowning. "Sorry?"

She shrugged. "What if I do want to stick with you?" she said and then laughed. "Sounds wrong but gets the idea across."

He grinned. "It's also pretty clear, and I'll never argue with that. And I hope you do," he replied quietly. "I wondered these last few days because it seemed like you wanted to be just friends."

"More than friends," she murmured. "I'm already trying to figure out what to do if you leave, like you were talking about a long-distance relationship. And I … I don't think I can handle that."

His face fell, and he nodded slowly. "I can understand that," he murmured. "It is definitely something I'm giving a lot of thought to."

"And do you have any answers?"

"Not yet," he said, "but I hope to soon."

She nodded slowly. "Maybe you could let me know when you get there?" she asked hopefully.

"I can do that," he replied. "It would help to know a little bit more about how you feel about everything."

"Well, I think I just said how I felt," she murmured.

He nodded. "True enough." Yet his voice was a little distant, a little sad.

"Do you really have to go so far away?"

He shook his head. "I don't have to, no. I'm not even sure where I'm going," he murmured. "I have to come up with some kind of a career, something to do."

"And you have to do that right away?"

"No," he admitted thoughtfully. "I'm friends with a guy who used to be here as a patient, and he has opened a center in town that helps veterans adjust to their new civilian lives."

"Right, I heard about that," she said. "I'm not sure which one of the guys did that, but I'm sure Dani could tell you more about it."

He nodded. "Maybe I should talk to him first, see what

kind of options there are in town."

"And do you have a problem living in Texas?"

"Nope," he replied, "not if there's a reason for it. I don't want to just make an arbitrary decision, if I need to be somewhere else."

She nodded. "And I can see that too, but I hope that you don't."

"It means a lot to you to stay in Dallas?"

"It means a lot to me to stay here at Hathaway House. Maybe that's a little hard for you to understand. I don't know, but this feels very much like family for me, very much like it's where I belong."

"And it's pretty hard to argue with that too. Obviously we have things to think about."

"We do," she murmured. And that was the end of that.

AFTER LANA LEFT, Ryatt remained at the pool for a long time, just sitting with the cup of coffee that she had brought him. It had long gone cold, but he didn't care. When he got chilled, he moved over to the hot tub and sat there, lost in thought. When Dennis came around and nudged him gently, Ryatt looked up, startled. "Sorry. I was lost in the clouds."

"Or lost in love," Dennis noted, with a bright smile.

Ryatt gave him a wry lip twitch. "I don't know. Nothing's ever quite so smooth in that department."

"It's not meant to be," Dennis declared, still smiling. "It's supposed to be something that you have to work through."

"Why is that?" Ryatt murmured. "Shouldn't it be easy?"

When he realized Ryatt meant this as a serious question, Dennis replied, "I don't know. I understand why we're supposed to work at it, so that we learn to appreciate a little more," he murmured, "but I don't really understand what your problem is with that."

"Well, the problem is," he explained, "I just don't understand how to get this the way I want it."

"I think the whole point is," Dennis added, "that you're supposed to figure out your own heart and then go after what your heart wants."

Ryatt smiled. "Now if only it were that easy."

"I'm not sure it's *not* that easy," Dennis countered. "It's obvious the two of you have something going on."

"And yet," Ryatt murmured, "it feels like we don't really get anywhere."

"Depends where you're wanting to go," he murmured.

"I guess. We're always talking around in circles."

"And I'm sure you are because it seems like that's just what people do instead of communicating and letting go of the fear of expressing themselves."

"How did you know it was fear-based?" Ryatt asked, with a groan.

"It seems like everything's about fear."

"Yep, that sure is what I'm working on," Ryatt shared. "Everything from being afraid that the program that I'm with will fail, and I'll end up having to come back, just like my sister did. And that's pretty hard to even contemplate. Add to that failing at a future career and having to start all over again, plus failing at this relationship and losing what's important."

"Of course your relationship is important," Dennis said, "but why would you even consider that your PT program could fail?"

"It just seems like, if Quinton didn't have to come back, it would seem like it was a success, but, because she did have to return, it feels like it's not a success."

"It sounds to me like you need to work on your definition of what is a success or what is a fail."

"Yeah, you're not the only one who has suggested that to me," he murmured. "In my sister's case, I just think that it would probably have been a lot easier for her to not need to come back."

"And what? Let Quinton remain in pain and deteriorate further? No. You keep trying to get better. So you return to the program. Also, you have to consider that she and Stan wouldn't have got together again."

Ryatt stared at Dennis. "So do you think things like that are arranged by fate or destiny or whatever, just so that they get together?"

"That appeals to my romantic heart," Dennis said, with a smile. "Do I understand how and what? No, I don't, but what I do understand is that, when it's right, it's right. And you should know that in your heart. And, if it isn't right, then you should also know that too."

"It feels right," Ryatt said hesitantly.

"Sure, but you haven't got to the point of *saying* it is right. You're still stuck on the I-*think*-it's-right level."

"Well, how do you know for sure?"

"The only thing that's stopping you," Dennis guessed, "is the fact that, in your mind, she hasn't confirmed how she feels, and that's the only reason that you're unsure."

"That's quite true, although it would be a lot easier if she did confirm."

"But have you asked her?"

"No, not yet," Ryatt said. "I'm … We've talked around it many times. About, you know, the future and long-distance relationships and all that good stuff." He gave Dennis a half smile. "But not getting to the heart of the matter."

"And again that's fear," Dennis stated quietly. "And you don't have to stay stuck at that level."

"Are you sure?" Ryatt joked, with a twitch of his lips. "Seems like a nice safe place to be."

"Sure, but, when you went into the military, that wasn't a safe job. When you went out on assignment, where you had to rescue your team member, that wasn't a safe trip. When you came here, and you took a chance on Quinton's advice, that wasn't a safe trip. Since when are you so stuck on *safe* that you forget about the joys of taking a chance and following your heart?"

Ryatt stared at Dennis. "I hadn't considered it that way."

"Of course not. You're letting fear paralyze you, and that's not the man who I understood was here," Dennis noted quietly. "I mean, you're welcome to be that other man. I'm not saying that you can't be, but that hesitant you doesn't appear to me to be anything like the man I have known this last little while."

"No, I'm not," Ryatt admitted. "I would never have said I was a coward."

"Well, I certainly won't use that word," Dennis said, "because that implies something much harsher. However, I do think that you want to be seen as a man who can do things, who can face fears, who doesn't hide away."

"Yes, of course that's how I prefer to act, how I want to be seen," he replied in amazement.

After Dennis was gone, his words certainly gave Ryatt

something to think about, something that he hadn't yet expected. When Dennis had put it that way, it was quite true. Ryatt had been the person who stepped up and went back to rescue his friends; that's how Ryatt had been injured. And he would do it all over again. His friend Joe was alive. *So am I*, Ryatt reminded himself, and that's because of his actions that day.

Peter wasn't here still, and that was something Ryatt would have to live with. He certainly didn't want to go through life afraid that, given another opportunity, he wouldn't make the same choice. That wasn't living to him. That was being crippled by fear. And that's what Dennis was trying to say.

Ryatt wondered if Lana knew as many details about his accident as Dennis seemed to know. Ryatt wanted to tell her about it, so she heard it from him. So there were no secrets between them. So she knew that any subject could be spoken of with him. So she understood the guilt he still carried— should it come up in other forms within their relationship. However, he wasn't ready for that discussion. Not yet. Later.

RYATT THOUGHT ABOUT it a lot into the night, and the next morning he woke up, already late.

He worked his way through his morning PT exercises, trying to get as far as he could, as fast as he could, until Shane finally said, "Hey, what's the matter?"

Ryatt looked at him. "Just in a hurry today."

"Oh, I get it," Shane confirmed. "I'm just not sure why."

Ryatt shrugged. "I want to talk to Lana."

"Well, you can, can't you? At lunchtime? After work?"

"Probably. We don't really get a ton of time to talk. And often I'm too tired to make good use of the time."

"You're not that tired today though, are you?"

"No, I'm not," he murmured, "which is a good thing." And, at that, Shane called his session over. Ryatt headed back to his room and got a quick shower, before checking if Lana was in her office and ready for lunch. However, he saw no sign of her. He poked his head into Dani's office. "Is she here today?"

"No," she said. "She's out all day."

He frowned at that. "Is she okay?"

"Yes," Dani replied cheerfully. "Attending a one-day conference in town."

He nodded slowly. "Okay," he murmured, heading on down to the cafeteria to get his lunch.

Dennis saw him and raised an eyebrow. "You're alone. Not sure if that's good or bad," he murmured.

"She didn't come in today," Ryatt said quietly.

"Ah, well, that can put a kibosh on your day, but don't let it keep a kibosh on your life."

Ryatt nodded. "Wasn't planning on it. Not exactly sure what I'm planning on doing anyway."

"That's fine," Dennis agreed. "I'm sure when she comes in, you'll have lots of time to talk." And he quickly served him a meal and moved on to the guy behind him in line.

Ryatt hoped they did have time to talk; he really hoped that he had a chance to talk to Lana about some specific items, but it felt weird that he'd finally geared himself up to do this, and then she wasn't here. Wasn't that so typical. By the time he got through the rest of the day, he was tired and frustrated. He sent her a text message, asking if she was okay.

She immediately sent back a response. **Sorry, should**

have let you know I wasn't coming in today. Attending a conference with lots of speakers, all good info.

THE NEXT MORNING at eight, he was already late for an appointment with one of his doctors, when Lana stopped by. He didn't have time to talk to her right now. "I'm glad you're back. I wasn't sure what to think when you didn't show up or text me."

"Just lots of speakers all day long," she noted quietly. "Lots of decisions and thought processes to consider."

"I know. Me too." He gave her the gentlest of smiles. "Unfortunately I can't talk. I've got to go. I'm already late for my appointment."

She immediately disappeared out into the hallway, calling back, "Go," she said. "Have fun."

He wasn't sure if *fun* was the right word for it, but, by the time he finished going through the lab tests that had been taken a few weeks earlier and talking to the doctor about his pain meds, et cetera, Ryatt was more impatient than ever to find a window of opportunity to talk to her. When he went to find out if she was ready to go for lunch today, she was on the computer, in some kind of online meeting.

She shook her head and frowned, then whispered, "I'll be tied up."

He nodded and just left. And the frustrations just seemed to continue. As long as he had plans to try and talk to her, it seemed like the world had conspired against him. By the time the end of the day rolled around, he realized he still hadn't had a chance to talk to her. He sat on the side of his bed and wondered at his options. And realized that she was likely already gone for the day.

Plus, he didn't want to return to her office to talk to her for the third time today. Tired and depressed, he stayed alone in his room, wondering at the events hindering him, now that he had made this particular decision to speak to Lana.

RYATT WOKE UP the next morning to a knock on his door. "Come in."

Lana burst into his room. "We need to talk. I don't know what's going on, but, every time I try to talk to you, it seems like I just can't get a moment free."

He slowly pushed himself up in the bed. "Well, I would say the same thing to you," he agreed, with a half smile. He brushed his hair from his eyes and tried to wake up. "What time is it?"

She winced. "Early. I came in a half hour earlier to work, hoping that maybe we could talk."

"And that's possible. It just depends on the time limits we have for talking. However, could I at least get up, go to the bathroom, and maybe brush my teeth?"

She winced. "Look. You do that. I'll go grab us some coffee, and I'll bring it back." And, with that, she rushed out.

He was happy that she was here and possibly in a position where they could talk, but her timing was definitely a little on the early side. He'd had a horrible night and even now wasn't quite feeling himself. But, as he had a short window here to spend with her, he got up, made his way to the bathroom, gave his face a good scrub, and then stepped out after using the facilities. Back at his bed, he sat down and pulled on a pair of comfortable sports pants and a muscle shirt. At least he was somewhat dressed. By the time she returned, he was sitting on the bed, pushed up against the headboard and relaxing, wondering what she would talk about.

When she burst in, she took one look and smiled. "Good, at least you're up and moving."

"Yep, I am." He accepted the coffee, faced her, and asked, "Now what's going on?"

She frowned. "It just seems like every time we try to talk, we get interrupted. I was getting so frustrated."

"I was too," he murmured. "I just wasn't expecting you to show up this early."

She shrugged. "As I said, I got frustrated."

He burst out laughing. "Well, that's good to know. If it happens again, I'll know how to handle it."

She smiled. "I'm sorry. I probably should have waited and given you a chance to wake up on your own." She winced. "Are you mad at me?"

"No, of course not. When a beautiful woman wants to talk to me, why would I be mad?"

She smiled even bigger at those words. "I'm glad." She sat down on the single chair in the room and asked, "What are we doing with our lives?"

"I think we're moving forward," he said cautiously, not sure what she was trying to say.

She didn't say anything for a moment, just nodded and sipped her coffee.

"Unless you're trying to say that you want to go in a different direction." He frowned, trying to figure out just what was bothering her.

"The only direction I want to move is forward."

"Good," he said, with a note of relief. "That's exactly what I want."

She looked at him, smiled, and asked, "Do you think we want the same thing?"

"I don't know, but I sure hope so," he replied. "I'm not exactly sure what the problem is though."

"It isn't a problem, but I felt this urgency to discuss it with you," she noted. "I'm working on all this lovely fear stuff."

"You and me both," he winced. "And it just seems to be no end of it."

"I know. Me too."

Ryatt asked her, "What are you afraid of?"

"Of being an old maid, of not having a family, of not finding my one true love," she murmured. "I know it may sound stupid, and I don't mean it to, but it's a hardship for me, dealing with the fear of losing someone again, making me so afraid to commit because of that fear of loss. It's not something I'd ever really looked at before, and I'm not really sure how big an issue it is, but the people here? ... They are so strong and courageous that it makes me feel even worse for not confronting my fears. I'm dealing with grief over my mom and a weird sense of abandonment over my dad, but that's nothing compared to what everyone here is dealing with."

"Still, you are entitled to your feelings. And what about leaving here?"

"It would not be my choice, but, if that's the only answer, then"—she took a deep breath—"then yes."

He smiled. "That's interesting too. And I'm glad to hear that, but I don't think it'll be necessary."

She stared. "What do you mean?"

"I mean, there's a good chance I can find work locally."

She beamed. "If we could try to find work locally, I would love that." She added, "I really don't want to leave here. I really like my work at Hathaway."

"It's a valuable job, but the thing is, I don't really have any money to support a family."

"And you certainly wouldn't have to, not by yourself," she said. "I wasn't planning on quitting."

He chuckled. "You realize that we're getting all these details out of the way, but we haven't had *that talk*."

"I know. We keep avoiding it."

"Because nobody wants to be the first one to speak up."

She winced and nodded. "It is a little … difficult to be the first."

"And that's because we have to open ourselves up to the hurt, in case it's not what we're expecting it to be."

She nodded again. "I know." She took a deep breath. "And it seems foolish, but that's where it's at." And then she smiled at him. "But I tell you what, if you start, I'll follow." He burst out laughing, and she grinned. "See? We're good together."

"We are good together," he agreed warmly. "And we'll be even better together as time goes on."

She looked at him hopefully. "Do you think so?"

"I know so." He opened his arms and said, "I could use a hug."

She immediately put down her coffee, walked over, and gave him a hug. They held on to each other for a long moment, and then she stepped back and smiled at him. "I'm really glad I came for coffee this morning."

He laughed. "Me too. But you don't get to leave just yet,

as we haven't addressed the big first step."

"No," she murmured, as she looked down at her feet. She hitched her hip on the side of his bed and smiled. "Brings us back to the same thing."

"Sure, fear. You're afraid of all kinds of things, and so am I. However, I won't be the person who wishes I had said something when I had the opportunity, yet I didn't." He took a deep breath. "And speaking of fear, there's something I need to tell you. Maybe it will help you to understand some of the issues I've been dealing with." In a low tone he told her about Peter and what had happened and how the decision he'd made had tormented him ever since. When he finally fell silent, he looked up hesitantly to see her reaction. His heart jumped when he saw the tears welling in Lana's eyes.

She leaned closer and clasped her palms on either side of his face, still crying. "It wasn't your fault. That's a horrible decision that no one should have to make. You made the right one. I'm so sorry Peter died, but his death is not on you."

He nodded. "That's what my doctor said."

She nodded. "Good. I'm so sorry you went through all that. I can also certainly understand the doubt in your decision, but making peace with that and moving forward is the best thing you can do for yourself."

"And that's the point I've come to as well. I'll always carry Peter and that time in my heart and ache with the loss. He was a vibrant young man who died too young." His lips firmed up for a moment. "Of course that's not all I wanted to say but I figured, if I could get that out, the rest would be easier."

And he fell silent, as the words choked up inside him.

After a moment, she leaned closer, looking directly into his eyes. "So what is it you want to say?"

"Oh, I don't know," he joked, then let the words flow. "How about the fact that I love you, that I'd love to be at your side while you're rounded with my child, and I'd love for you to hold my hand through the ups as we age together, and I'd love for you to be the person who sits beside me on the front porch, when we're both old and gray—staring down at the years behind of us, smiling, because it's been such a great ride, and looking forward to the years ahead of us."

She looked up at him, and more tears were in her eyes. "You love me?"

Ryatt reached up a hand, gently brushed the tears off her cheeks. "Of course I don't know for sure that that's what you want."

"I love you too. And that's what I want more than anything, a life spent with you," she whispered. "I hadn't even considered it in that light."

"That's because not all of life is that simple or that easy." He smiled. "As it's been pointed out to me recently," he murmured, "an awful lot of hardships and ups and downs have to be gone through in life, but I want to be that guy who steps up and is prepared to do what's needed to be done," he murmured. "So I won't always be right, and I won't always be wrong," he said, with a laugh. "Yet I will have my fair share of being both."

"Nobody needs to always be right," she whispered, brushing tears from her eyes. "And nobody can be expected to always be right. It's too much stress on anybody," she murmured. "All we have to do is try to be the best that we can be at any time."

"And some people would say that's a very simplistic way to go through life," he murmured.

"Maybe," she agreed. "However, that's not a bad way to look at it or to go through life, in my opinion. We all need help sometimes. We all need something to make us feel better when we're down. Often it's just the confirmation that we're loved."

"That's true," he murmured, "but I think, more than that, we all need somebody else. We need somebody to hold us in the evening, to share a sunset to look at, to hold us in the morning when we wake up, to see something special in the dawn, or to share a thought that suddenly hits our brain cells when we're talking to somebody. I want to reach for that special person—you—to explain what's so special about that earlier thought and why it's so special that you are here and are listening and understand," he murmured, studying her quietly for a long moment, before he continued.

"I don't think love is something that needs to be breathtaking or earth-shattering. I think it can be that quiet smile inside your heart when you see someone," he murmured, reaching up to gently brush more tears dripping down her cheek. "I think it needs to be that extra-special thing that you can't define with words because it chokes you up from the inside, and it makes you realize that you have no other way to express it or to explain just how it feels. Plus, it should be an inner knowing that accepts people aren't perfect and that we're all in a state of becoming," he murmured, "that every day some of us will make mistakes, and every day some of us will do something great or have the potential to do something great. It's a matter of having patience and tolerance and acceptance."

She looked up and smiled. "I think we can handle that."

"I'd like to think so," he said, with a gentle smile. "I haven't done all that great so far. But I know that every day is an opportunity for change, every day is an opportunity to do better, and every day is an opportunity to show you how much I care." He brushed her cheek gently.

She smiled. "What makes you think I need more than that?" She clasped his hand. "I didn't expect to find a relationship here," she murmured. "Honestly I just … I've seen so many patients come and go, and I thought they were all so truly blessed, when I saw the relationships happen along with the medical successes. Sure, a part of me was a little jealous. A part of me wished I had somebody with me, but it wasn't something that I was actively looking for. And then you showed up, and you were cranky and miserable, and you basically kicked me out of your room." She grinned broadly. "And I knew that something was very different about you. Everybody here is always upbeat and positive, but you were just the real you. And I had to appreciate that."

"I don't ever expect to be a perfect husband," he murmured. "I know I'm as flawed as the next man, but I can tell you one thing." He paused, focused on her fully. "I promise I'll love you every day of your life, and I'll cherish every moment we have together." She shook her head, and his heart froze. He sucked in his breath and waited …

When she realized what he'd assumed, she immediately cried out, "That's not what I meant. I just can't imagine that you would ever be anything other than that. It's been so special to have you in my life in this short span of time," she explained, "that I want to make sure that we cherish all the time that we do have together."

He nodded. "I'm with you there." And he grinned. "But for a moment …"

She threw her arms around him and held him close. "Nope, no *for a moment here*. Maybe I thought this was what would happen when I came in this morning. I don't know. I do know that I was pretty desperate to have some answers."

Ryatt nodded. "Me too. I figured fear was keeping me back, and fear was possibly keeping you back. Then somebody mentioned to me what I was like when I was active military, and how fear was not something I allowed to hold me back, and I agreed. I realized that that's exactly what I was doing, and I didn't want to be that person anymore, which is why I've been trying to get a hold of you for the last few days. Yet it seemed like we were constantly being interrupted."

"As if life conspired against us," she murmured.

He smiled, pulled her close, and whispered, "But no more."

She nodded. "We'll have a lot of explaining to do here though."

"No, we won't." He laughed. "Everyone at Hathaway House is already expecting it. What we'll need is some patience in order to get me out of here."

"I'm not in any rush for that," she murmured. "I need you as healthy and as strong as you can be. And, no, not for my sake but for yours." He stared fondly at her, as she continued. "You think I don't know that it's important to you that you be as fit and as strong and as healthy as you can be? Because I know it is. You keep thinking it's for me, but it's not. It's for you."

He nodded. "I had to learn that too. To stop looking at doing things for other people but to do them because it was the right thing to do for me. Nobody will be surprised about our relationship," he added, "but they'll all be happy for us."

"Not quite as happy as I will be." Then she stopped, frowned. "What about your sister?"

"She'll be even happier. And I want to get on my feet and in much better shape, so I can walk her down the aisle, and then it'll be our turn."

She looked up at him and whispered, "You haven't asked me."

His eyebrows shot up, as if suddenly realizing that he'd missed something, and he nodded. "You're right." And he had missed something; he just hadn't gotten that far. She'd thrown everything off-kilter.

He gently held her chin between his fingers and whispered, "Lana, would you do me the honor of becoming my wife, becoming the mother of my children, and holding my hand through thick and thin, being there through all the years that we may be blessed to have together?" he murmured. "And accept me when I fail, offer your hand when I need help, and be there when I feel alone? And I promise I'll do the same."

With more tears in her eyes, she whispered, "Yes, dear God, yes."

He laughed and pulled her into his arms and held her close. Life had never looked better.

Epilogue

SPENCER NEWCOMB SHARED a semiprivate VA hospital room with his friend Timothy Watkins. "I don't get it," Spencer said. "Why are you trying to get into this place so much?"

"Because it's got a fantastic rep," Timothy murmured. "And this place sucks."

Well, Spencer wouldn't argue with that assessment of their current scenario because, well, it was true. There was an awful lot that they didn't like about it here.

Timothy added, "And you and I are a team. We've been through so much already, and we should stick together in healing as well."

"And what makes you think this Hathaway place will be any better?"

"How can it be worse?"

"It's still a long trip for nothing."

"Or it could be a long trip for everything," Timothy argued. "You know, in some of the online forums, the guys talk about the different methods the guys at Hathaway House have of getting people back on their feet. I'm willing to try." He frowned. "I think some of your friends went there too."

Spencer rolled his head toward Timothy and asked, "Yeah, who?"

"Percy, for one."

Spencer's eyebrows shot up at that.

Timothy continued. "Ha, and didn't you know Lance?"

"Well, I know *a* Lance," Spencer replied. "Doesn't mean I know the one who you're talking about."

"No, that's true, but I think you'd probably do some good to ask them. Then fill me in, but I'm already sold. We both should sign up. You never know. You might get into this place before I do, knowing Percy and Lance."

"And maybe not," Spencer argued, with a smile. "After all, it's not as if I'll necessarily jump ahead in line. You know, if a place is this good, it'll have a queue waiting to get in."

"Yeah, it sure will," Timothy agreed. "I'm just filling out the application now, but you know how I hate all this paperwork and dredging up all my medical history. Why do they want us to list all this stuff on their stupid forms when they also want our medical reports? Such a waste to ask for things twice." Shaking his head, Timothy was typing on his phone. "I sent you the link. Maybe if you're dealing with this headache of paperwork too, I'll be happier dealing with my application."

Spencer's phone beeped, and he looked at the link on his screen, still undecided.

Timothy nodded at his buddy. "Try it. I mean, what's the harm?"

After Timothy headed off for his therapy session, Spencer looked again at the link and frowned. It sounded a little bit too good to be true. It had been a really long time since Spencer got taken in by a dream, but it did seem to him that, if there were any truth to the Hathaway hype, some of his friends who already did their rehab there might very well give him answers, one way or the other.

So Spencer sent off a couple emails and followed up a

couple text messages. When Lance got back to him and said, *If you get an opportunity, go,* Spencer was really surprised. Then he got an email back from Percy, saying, *Go, man, go.* After that, Spencer filled out the application without another thought. He told Timothy to get his butt in gear and finish his application too. Spencer's internal critic highly expected to not get in; a place like that would have a long waiting list.

Nobody was more surprised than him and even Timothy when, just two days later, Spencer got an email response from Hathaway House, asking for more medical records. Spencer quickly filled out everything that needed to be done and then sent it all off, nudging Timothy once more to get the lead out. "We're partners in this. I need my partner on this leg of the journey."

Timothy nodded, but Spencer didn't see his buddy jumping online.

When Spencer got a phone call not very long afterward, it was from the manager of the center. She introduced herself and said, "I'm calling about your wish to join Hathaway House."

"Well, I was … I had … I know both Percy and Lance," he muttered.

"They do give you glowing references," she noted quietly. "We do prefer to take people who understand just how different we are here," she murmured.

"I don't know how different you are, but I can tell you that, in all the other rehab places I've been, nobody's ever given me a good recommendation for any of them."

She laughed. "No, and it's not an easy road that you guys are on," she stated, "which is one of the reasons why we try hard to make your stay here as pleasant and as productive as possible. I do have an opening, but it will be in about six weeks. … Wait. Let me check on that. Hang on a minute."

She came back a few minutes later and said, "I have a cancellation. I could move you up to three weeks."

"Wow. Seriously?"

"Yes. You just tell me if you want to proceed and arrange for your departure accordingly, and then I need to contact your doctors. We have to start that whole transfer procedure. Your treating physicians must give their permission for you and your records to be moved. In which case the three-week opening could be too tight."

Spencer frowned at that. "I don't know if they'll go for it," he noted, "but I would like to try."

"Good enough," she said. "Leave it in my hands, and I'll get back to you, when I find out a date that we're good to go." And, with that, she hung up.

When Spencer just asked Timothy about the status of his application, he moaned. "Man, you know how I feel about filling out this application. I got started, and I didn't get any further."

"Right, but maybe you want to now," Spencer added, "since I already got in."

Timothy looked at him, stunned. "What? What do you mean?" he cried out in dismay. "I only told you about it a few days ago."

"She just called me," he said, motioning at the phone. "She'll get the process started. She had a cancellation, and I can get in three weeks from now. Apparently it'll take that long to get everything together."

In shock, his friend collapsed onto his bed beside Spencer's.

"Get your application in," Spencer urged. "You never know. We could go at the same time."

And that was finally enough for Timothy to jump on board. "I'd better," he snapped. "I can't believe you got in before me."

"You took too long," Spencer stated bluntly. "You can't talk about these places and their queues. You have to make a decision and jump."

"Since when did you ever jump?" he muttered.

"Hey, you might be surprised." Spencer laughed. "Sometimes I don't need to be persuaded. I can see a good thing in front of me."

"Says you," he protested. "I'm still in shock."

"Well, deal with it," Spencer murmured, "because I'm going. Anything to get out of here will be better than where we are."

"Exactly." Timothy looked up and asked, "If I don't get in right away, you'll let me know what it's like, right?"

"Absolutely." Spencer smiled at his friend. "And you may want to pass it around that there's another option too. We've got a lot of friends here who could use a chance to get out and to get something better."

"I know," he murmured. "I'll do that. I'll start drumming up some more interest in the Hathaway place—but not until I get my spot secured," he declared. "No way will anybody else jump that line on me."

At that, Spencer shook his head. "Then jump in again. You were too slow to fill out the application. I just did what you said."

"Wow, I won't be slow anymore," Timothy muttered. And right then and there he finished it and submitted the form. "Done now," he announced. "and hopefully I can get in too."

This concludes Book 19 of Hathaway House: Ryatt.

Read about Spencer: Hathaway House, Book 19

Hathaway House: Spencer (Book #19)

***Welcome to Hathaway House. Rehab Center. Safe Haven.
Second chance at life and love.***

Getting into Hathaway House before his friend wasn't the plan, but that's how it worked out, leaving Spencer in a state of waiting for his buddy to arrive. In the meantime, he has work to do. Right from day one he wants to establish and to maintain some independence in this way-too-busy center, luckily meeting the groundskeeper on his first attempt at getting coffee.

Bella has been looking after the Hathaway House grounds for over five years. Although she's seen and interacted with many of the residents here, she never really got close to any—until Spencer. Now she can't help but watch his progress in awe, as he moves through his program with dedication. Is he trying so hard to show off to his soon-to-arrive friend? Or for her sake? Or because he's eager to leave the center and start his new improved future?

A future that won't be in Hathaway House and one that might not include her ...

Find Book 19 here!

To find out more visit Dale Mayer's website.

https://geni.us/DMSpencerUniversal

Author's Note

Thank you for reading Ryatt: Hathaway House, Book 18! If you enjoyed the book, please take a moment and leave a short review.

Dear reader,

I love to hear from readers, and you can contact me at my website: www.dalemayer.com or at my Facebook author page. To be informed of new releases and special offers, sign up for my newsletter or follow me on BookBub. And if you are interested in joining Dale Mayer's Reader Group, here is the Facebook sign up page.
http://geni.us/DaleMayerFBGroup

Cheers,
Dale Mayer

About the Author

Dale Mayer is a *USA Today* best-selling author, best known for her SEALs military romances, her Psychic Visions series, and her Lovely Lethal Garden cozy series. Her contemporary romances are raw and full of passion and emotion (Broken But ... Mending, Hathaway House series). Her thrillers will keep you guessing (Kate Morgan, By Death series), and her romantic comedies will keep you giggling (*It's a Dog's Life*, a stand-alone novella; and the Broken Protocols series, starring Charming Marvin, the cat).

Dale honors the stories that come to her—and some of them are crazy, break all the rules and cross multiple genres!

To go with her fiction, she also writes nonfiction in many different fields, with books available on résumé writing, companion gardening, and the US mortgage system. All her books are available in print and ebook format.

Connect with Dale Mayer Online

Dale's Website – www.dalemayer.com
Twitter – @DaleMayer
Facebook Page – geni.us/DaleMayerFBFanPage
Facebook Group – geni.us/DaleMayerFBGroup
BookBub – geni.us/DaleMayerBookbub
Instagram – geni.us/DaleMayerInstagram
Goodreads – geni.us/DaleMayerGoodreads
Newsletter – geni.us/DaleNews

Also by Dale Mayer

Published Adult Books:

Shadow Recon
Magnus, Book 1

Bullard's Battle
Ryland's Reach, Book 1
Cain's Cross, Book 2
Eton's Escape, Book 3
Garret's Gambit, Book 4
Kano's Keep, Book 5
Fallon's Flaw, Book 6
Quinn's Quest, Book 7
Bullard's Beauty, Book 8
Bullard's Best, Book 9
Bullard's Battle, Books 1–2
Bullard's Battle, Books 3–4
Bullard's Battle, Books 5–6
Bullard's Battle, Books 7–8

Terkel's Team
Damon's Deal, Book 1
Wade's War, Book 2
Gage's Goal, Book 3
Calum's Contact, Book 4
Rick's Road, Book 5
Scott's Summit, Book 6

Brody's Beast, Book 7
Terkel's Twist, Book 8

Kate Morgan
Simon Says... Hide, Book 1
Simon Says... Jump, Book 2
Simon Says... Ride, Book 3
Simon Says... Scream, Book 4
Simon Says... Run, Book 5

Hathaway House
Aaron, Book 1
Brock, Book 2
Cole, Book 3
Denton, Book 4
Elliot, Book 5
Finn, Book 6
Gregory, Book 7
Heath, Book 8
Iain, Book 9
Jaden, Book 10
Keith, Book 11
Lance, Book 12
Melissa, Book 13
Nash, Book 14
Owen, Book 15
Percy, Book 16
Quinton, Book 17
Ryatt, Book 18
Spencer, Book 19
Hathaway House, Books 1–3
Hathaway House, Books 4–6
Hathaway House, Books 7–9

The K9 Files
Ethan, Book 1
Pierce, Book 2
Zane, Book 3
Blaze, Book 4
Lucas, Book 5
Parker, Book 6
Carter, Book 7
Weston, Book 8
Greyson, Book 9
Rowan, Book 10
Caleb, Book 11
Kurt, Book 12
Tucker, Book 13
Harley, Book 14
Kyron, Book 15
Jenner, Book 16
Rhys, Book 17
Landon, Book 18
The K9 Files, Books 1–2
The K9 Files, Books 3–4
The K9 Files, Books 5–6
The K9 Files, Books 7–8
The K9 Files, Books 9–10
The K9 Files, Books 11–12

Lovely Lethal Gardens
Arsenic in the Azaleas, Book 1
Bones in the Begonias, Book 2
Corpse in the Carnations, Book 3
Daggers in the Dahlias, Book 4
Evidence in the Echinacea, Book 5

Footprints in the Ferns, Book 6
Gun in the Gardenias, Book 7
Handcuffs in the Heather, Book 8
Ice Pick in the Ivy, Book 9
Jewels in the Juniper, Book 10
Killer in the Kiwis, Book 11
Lifeless in the Lilies, Book 12
Murder in the Marigolds, Book 13
Nabbed in the Nasturtiums, Book 14
Offed in the Orchids, Book 15
Poison in the Pansies, Book 16
Quarry in the Quince, Book 17
Revenge in the Roses, Book 18
Silenced in the Sunflowers, Book 19
Lovely Lethal Gardens, Books 1–2
Lovely Lethal Gardens, Books 3–4
Lovely Lethal Gardens, Books 5–6
Lovely Lethal Gardens, Books 7–8
Lovely Lethal Gardens, Books 9–10

Psychic Vision Series
Tuesday's Child
Hide 'n Go Seek
Maddy's Floor
Garden of Sorrow
Knock Knock...
Rare Find
Eyes to the Soul
Now You See Her
Shattered
Into the Abyss
Seeds of Malice

Eye of the Falcon
Itsy-Bitsy Spider
Unmasked
Deep Beneath
From the Ashes
Stroke of Death
Ice Maiden
Snap, Crackle…
What If…
Talking Bones
String of Tears
Psychic Visions Books 1–3
Psychic Visions Books 4–6
Psychic Visions Books 7–9

By Death Series
Touched by Death
Haunted by Death
Chilled by Death
By Death Books 1–3

Broken Protocols – Romantic Comedy Series
Cat's Meow
Cat's Pajamas
Cat's Cradle
Cat's Claus
Broken Protocols 1-4

Broken and… Mending
Skin
Scars
Scales (of Justice)
Broken but… Mending 1-3

Glory
Genesis
Tori
Celeste
Glory Trilogy

Biker Blues
Morgan: Biker Blues, Volume 1
Cash: Biker Blues, Volume 2

SEALs of Honor
Mason: SEALs of Honor, Book 1
Hawk: SEALs of Honor, Book 2
Dane: SEALs of Honor, Book 3
Swede: SEALs of Honor, Book 4
Shadow: SEALs of Honor, Book 5
Cooper: SEALs of Honor, Book 6
Markus: SEALs of Honor, Book 7
Evan: SEALs of Honor, Book 8
Mason's Wish: SEALs of Honor, Book 9
Chase: SEALs of Honor, Book 10
Brett: SEALs of Honor, Book 11
Devlin: SEALs of Honor, Book 12
Easton: SEALs of Honor, Book 13
Ryder: SEALs of Honor, Book 14
Macklin: SEALs of Honor, Book 15
Corey: SEALs of Honor, Book 16
Warrick: SEALs of Honor, Book 17
Tanner: SEALs of Honor, Book 18
Jackson: SEALs of Honor, Book 19
Kanen: SEALs of Honor, Book 20
Nelson: SEALs of Honor, Book 21
Taylor: SEALs of Honor, Book 22

Colton: SEALs of Honor, Book 23
Troy: SEALs of Honor, Book 24
Axel: SEALs of Honor, Book 25
Baylor: SEALs of Honor, Book 26
Hudson: SEALs of Honor, Book 27
Lachlan: SEALs of Honor, Book 28
Paxton: SEALs of Honor, Book 29
SEALs of Honor, Books 1–3
SEALs of Honor, Books 4–6
SEALs of Honor, Books 7–10
SEALs of Honor, Books 11–13
SEALs of Honor, Books 14–16
SEALs of Honor, Books 17–19
SEALs of Honor, Books 20–22
SEALs of Honor, Books 23–25

Heroes for Hire
Levi's Legend: Heroes for Hire, Book 1
Stone's Surrender: Heroes for Hire, Book 2
Merk's Mistake: Heroes for Hire, Book 3
Rhodes's Reward: Heroes for Hire, Book 4
Flynn's Firecracker: Heroes for Hire, Book 5
Logan's Light: Heroes for Hire, Book 6
Harrison's Heart: Heroes for Hire, Book 7
Saul's Sweetheart: Heroes for Hire, Book 8
Dakota's Delight: Heroes for Hire, Book 9
Tyson's Treasure: Heroes for Hire, Book 10
Jace's Jewel: Heroes for Hire, Book 11
Rory's Rose: Heroes for Hire, Book 12
Brandon's Bliss: Heroes for Hire, Book 13
Liam's Lily: Heroes for Hire, Book 14
North's Nikki: Heroes for Hire, Book 15

SEALs of Steel

SEALs of Steel, Books 5–8
SEALs of Steel, Books 1–8

The Mavericks
Kerrick, Book 1
Griffin, Book 2
Jax, Book 3
Beau, Book 4
Asher, Book 5
Ryker, Book 6
Miles, Book 7
Nico, Book 8
Keane, Book 9
Lennox, Book 10
Gavin, Book 11
Shane, Book 12
Diesel, Book 13
Jerricho, Book 14
Killian, Book 15
Hatch, Book 16
Corbin, Book 17
Aiden, Book 18
The Mavericks, Books 1–2
The Mavericks, Books 3–4
The Mavericks, Books 5–6
The Mavericks, Books 7–8
The Mavericks, Books 9–10
The Mavericks, Books 11–12

Collections
Dare to Be You...
Dare to Love...
Dare to be Strong...

RomanceX3

Standalone Novellas
It's a Dog's Life
Riana's Revenge
Second Chances

Published Young Adult Books:

Family Blood Ties Series
Vampire in Denial
Vampire in Distress
Vampire in Design
Vampire in Deceit
Vampire in Defiance
Vampire in Conflict
Vampire in Chaos
Vampire in Crisis
Vampire in Control
Vampire in Charge
Family Blood Ties Set 1–3
Family Blood Ties Set 1–5
Family Blood Ties Set 4–6
Family Blood Ties Set 7–9
Sian's Solution, A Family Blood Ties Series Prequel
    Novelette

Design series
Dangerous Designs
Deadly Designs
Darkest Designs
Design Series Trilogy

Standalone

In Cassie's Corner

Gem Stone (a Gemma Stone Mystery)

Time Thieves

Published Non-Fiction Books:

Career Essentials

Career Essentials: The Résumé

Career Essentials: The Cover Letter

Career Essentials: The Interview

Career Essentials: 3 in 1

Printed in Great Britain
by Amazon

53120851R00108